Splatterpunk
Forever

A Charity Anthology

Edited by
Jack Bantry & Kit Power

Published by
SPLATTERPUNK ZINE

Cover illustration © 2018 Chris Enterline
Introduction © 2018 Glenn Rolfe

The Seacretor © 2018 Ryan Harding
Garrote © 2018 Lydian Faust
Junkyard Shift © 2018 Ryan C Thomas
Cougars © 2018 Sisters of Slaughter
Guinea Pig Blues © 2018 Chad Lutzke
Blood on the Walls © 2018 Saul Bailey
Chum © 2018 Nathan Robinson
The Bearded Woman © 2018 Alessandro Manzetti
Finger Paint © 2018 Robert Essig
Diamond in the Rough © 2018 JR Park
Virtue of Stagnant Water © 2018 Monica J O'Rourke

ISBN 9781730870163
Independently published

For the *Splatter Punks*

Contents

Acknowledgments

Jack Bantry: Thanks to Kit Power for co-editing this anthology, (your assistance is greatly appreciated!). Thanks to all the contributors for letting Kit and myself use (and trust us with) your stories in our anthology; Chris Enterline, for the super artwork; and Mike Dickinson, for once again doing the cover design. None of this would be possible without all of your generosity. And most importantly, thanks to YOU, the reader, for buying this book!

Kit Power: First, thanks so much to Jack Bantry for inviting me back for another round of Splatterpunk anthology insanity. It's an enormous privilege to be part of such a well loved and respected series, and I'm proud to be involved. Thanks, too, to all the amazingly talented storytellers who trusted us with their fantastic work. And thanks to all the readers who buy this series, devour these stories, tell their friends, and vote for award nominations (!!!). Your love and support is gobsmacking, and only spurs us on to greater efforts. We will never take you for granted.

As ever, thanks also to Jim Mcleod - Editor in Chief of Gingernuts Of Horror, for his continued support and friendship, and for being a true champion of the genre.

And finally, thanks as ever to my wife of 10 years, for continuing to support me in my many mad ventures. I love you so much.

Introduction

'Round Our Way

    Splatterpunk Forever!

    Man, that just sounds like a war cry, doesn't it? And it really does seem timely. There is a revelation going on in this world. Political sides are sticking to their guns even when they should be apologizing as if their asses depended on it. Social media freaks are twittering, re-tweeting, Facebook sharing, and swearing up a storm, right or wrong, Hell or high water, and most of them are clueless. We have people raging and clawing at one another in the streets and online... *Fear* is at an all-time high. *Fear* of ignorance. *Fear* that the things we love are being destroyed. *Fear* of an unknown future. That's on all sides. Conservatives are hemorrhaging over the changes in this world, and in our species. Tattoos, blue hair, boys with boys, girls with girls, gender-free restrooms! And the liberals are certain the chaos at the top is going to dismantle democracy and goodwill to our fellow man. In other words, the world is on edge.

It's upon that edge that the Splatterpunk horror we love was born. People were coming down from the sex and drugs of the seventies and crashing into an energy crisis thanks to the spark up of a war in the desert. In the eighties, the "gays" (oh my!) were coming out in droves and taking over our streets with parades and sex clubs. The Aids epidemic exploded seemingly from out of nowhere, and the blame game only pointed its finger in the direction of the gay community. Russia and America were still playing cold war games and holding their sweaty, power hungry paws over the red button. Women were working alongside men, but getting verbally accosted and raped in shitty little break rooms. Shit was on the verge of going nuclear.

In the middle of it all, came a story from a man they called Jack.

OFF SEASON by Jack Ketchum launched a new, raw, uncut, fearless fist to the face of storytelling that scared the bejesus out of readers everywhere. It launched the Splatterpunk movement in the horror literary world. The shocking story of a writer and her friends grabbing a cozy little cabin on the Maine coast only to be attacked and killed in a plethora of gruesome ways by a group of savages forgotten by society was brutal and relentless. For this, the book was met with controversy and had people crying about the depictions of extreme violence. America wanted to know why somebody would write something like this. Decades after its release, in an interview with ScFiNow in 2013, Ketchum mentioned wanting to write in the details that horror films of the day were allowed to use, and that horror literature, for some reason, wimped out on. Ketchum wanted to put characters in an impossibly horrible situation and see what happened. He said, "I wanted to ask, what would *you* do under these circumstances? How far would *you* go to survive?"

OFF SEASON came out in 1980. Here we are almost forty years later, and the world is as frenzied, scattered, and frightening as ever, no matter which side of the line you stand on. In other words, the world is ripe with fear and perfect for Splatterpunk. For us horror writers, it's a very cathartic way of dealing with the frustrations and anxiety, for you readers, it's an escape and a break from all of the fucked up things happening to and around you in real life.

Thanks to Kit Power and Jack Bantry, and the Splatterpunk charity anthologies such as the one you're holding now, it's time to get away from the atrocities of the day, big and small, imagined and real alike, and get into some dirty, bloody, in your face fiction. Key word: "fiction". You have our permission to kick back, relax, and get ready for some scary ass fun, motherfuckers.

Splatterpunk forever!!!!!

Glenn Rolfe
Summer, 2018

The Seacretor
Ryan Harding

1.

Grant fucked the tree on the sixth day.

I watched him do it from down below, near the massive letters we dug into the sand which spelled HELP. We did this on both sides of the island, which was thirsty work even when we worked in the shade. We didn't ration the water skillfully, which was why he and Tanya drank the tree jizz on day five.

I guess I'm getting ahead of myself, though, so let me back up.

2.

The *Seacretor* was Grant's boat.

I felt like the whole invitation was intended as an opportunity for Grant to play his demo reel for Tanya. You know, "All of this could be yours, if you just told Ben thanks but no thanks and took a hit of my dick instead." I don't think he wanted her initially, but she met both of us at the same party and started dating me, which wounded his ego. How could she choose the guy who couldn't have attended such a prestigious college without a lacrosse scholarship, had to work in the library on top of that and whose second hand car was four years old? What sorcery made me the better option than the trust fund prince with the hot shit dad whose load was one of the first to hit the floor during the Illuminati circle jerk? He was *Grant!*

We were barely friends, and only because I tutored him last semester. He could count how many houses his family owned (three) and on how many continents (two), but otherwise his math skills left much to be desired. An owl could solve a Rubik's cube before Grant managed to pass his courses on his own, so it was Ben to the rescue. Grant escaped with a C- average and I earned a summer invitation to his family estate on an island he said "you've probably never heard of." (Admittedly I hadn't. Tanya and I privately called it "the Island of Dr. Maroon" at first, but she stopped doing it when we got there.) I wasn't sure if Tanya and I would last, but neither of us planned to go back home for the whole summer, so the chance at a month-long vacation was hard to pass up.

The mansion was impressive, I'll admit, with a view to the beach from most every window, but an indoor pool too if you didn't feel like walking a whole three blocks. Tanya fell for it immediately. I was more reserved, waiting for a thirty minute head start to run for our lives before disaffected rich guys with pith helmets and elephant guns hunted us down.

After a week, Grant grew tired of the scenery, or at least he felt like he'd impressed Tanya as much as he could with his home, the beach, the scenic hikes, and the exclusive island club. He insisted we take out the *Seacretor* (he was way too proud of that name) for a few nights, get a taste of other islands and their posh restaurants, hotels, and cuisines.

I proved to be as adept with the sea as Grant was with equations. Lots of puking over the side into the Pacific. Bonus time for Grant and Tanya. I wondered if he purposely kept us out in the ocean longer when he saw what it did to me, and that may have been why we came across the island instead of docking a couple hours earlier when we had the chance.

I thought Grant was playing it up when he said the island wasn't charted on whatever deluxe mapping system he was using. He moved in for a closer look, with Tanya excited by the prospect of the adventure. A couple hundred yards out should have been enough to conclude nobody bothered mapping it because it sucked, but the *Seacretor* drifted closer as Grant and Tanya hyped this mystery island and I held my head in my hands and tried not to puke.

"I bet there's buried treasure," Tanya joked.

I was about to opine that Grant needed greater riches like R. Kelly needed a diuretic, and that's when a spire of rock smashed through the hull of the *Seacretor*. A few minutes later we stood drenched on the shore of the island after a hundred yard swim, each of us in sodden shirts and swimming trunks or bikini bottoms, all signs of our vessel erased like paint smeared over a landscape to hide a mistake.

3.

"I don't know where the hell that rock came from," Captain Fuckface swore as we took stock of our inventory—a hastily grabbed first-aid kit, flare gun case, a torpedo-sized bottle of water barely halfway full (my doing, after heaving my guts over the side), and a smartphone reluctant to power on after its dip in the ocean. MacGyver could build a submarine from that, but we'd be lucky if it meant a three day lease on life.

Tanya patted Grant on the arm as he stared at the site of the shipwreck, or the approximate spot, since it was hard to be sure now. It's no wonder boats and planes can disappear out here, swept under the globe's largest rug. We'd seen no other boats the past two hours since we drew away from the last island.

We were all alone.

If there was a silver lining to our predicament, it was that no expense would be spared on behalf of Grant's rescue. They'd send the armada for the golden boy and tell them to grab his friends, too, if there's room in a shipping crate.

We set down our supplies far from the surf and took stock of our environment. Yes, it was strange it did not appear on a mapping system—this was far more than some little outcropping of rock barely big enough for a sea gull orgy—but it wasn't much to look at from our current side. We saw a dwindling shoreline which ran alongside a column made of pure rock. This hill rose overhead roughly a hundred feet and stretched half a mile, kind of bony in appearance and unblemished by any trees or bushes on our side save for a lone tree at the top. I hoped that meant we'd find more signs of life on the other side of the rock.

Grant took the point to the nearest end of the island, far enough ahead to allow me a moment to talk privately with Tanya.

"I don't believe this," I said.

"Calm down. We'll be okay." Despite the assurance I thought she sounded annoyed with me, even though I wasn't the one who just crashed our ship and instantly cast the three of us in a remake of *Robinson Crusoe,* currently filming in the style of un-found footage.

"You don't think he should have paid more attention to the sonar than his bo-nar?"

Ten days ago she would have laughed until she snorted over that one, but now she rolled her eyes and walked faster until I was left alone with my shadow.

4.

I caught up to them at the end of the shoreline. The rock extended past the sand and we couldn't see all the way around to the other side. Waves exploded off its surface in bursts of white spume. Too easy to imagine a swimmer slammed into the wall repeatedly until sharks did him a favor and ate him.

"I bet it's the same on the other side," Grant said.

Well, he was certainly the authority today on obstacles we couldn't successfully negotiate, so I didn't argue. We walked back the way we came until we found a decent spot to ascend. It was more a punishing hike since we never truly climbed at any point. Ten minutes or so later we all stood by the tree, sucking wind.

The trunk had burst through the surface of stone, but for all its aspirations, it was a rather sorry excuse for a tree in the end. No leaves, no fronds, minimal shade. It looked like the withered three-fingered hand of a giant stick man.

"Yuck, what's that?" Tanya pointed to a limb on the far right. Something oozed from it, dark and syrup-like. She drew her hand away like she wouldn't be able to stop herself from touching it.

Grant smiled. "Bring any pancakes?"

Tanya tee-heed while I seethed; bo-nar was way funnier.

"Forget about the tree jizz." I gestured to notches in the trunk without sticking my fingers in them. "What's up with all these glory holes?"

Tanya's smile evaporated and her eyes went cloudward again. Grant shook his head like the joke was beneath him and brought us all down as human beings.

I examined the holes like I actually cared and Grant and Tanya were missing out on a sensational discovery. Each one opened to a disc of what I assumed was rotting bark and a true hole in the middle. I didn't pry since they glistened, probably from more of that fluid.

The top of the bluff stayed level twenty yards past the tree. We walked to the other side for essentially a mirror image of where we'd landed, except it had shade. After being in the direct sun for half an hour, we were ready for some of that. Otherwise it had nothing else we wanted or needed.

"This place sucks," Grant said.

"Yeah."

I wanted to remind them how excited they were about the island before. Their indifference now was too little, too late.

"There's nothing to eat." Tanya squinted as if we were overlooking a bucket of fried chicken somewhere. "Hey, is that a cave?"

She pointed. Turned out her eyes were good for more than just rolling at supremely funny jokes. Down and to the right in the shadier section of the rock was a protrusion that partially obstructed a deeper black. You could almost write it off as a shadow in the crag, but it was an opening for sure.

The path down required more care than the other side. Everyone made it fine, but we soon wished we hadn't bothered.

We all picked up stones before we entered the mouth, I guess in case we had to mount a coordinated effort to bludgeon a deadly cave parrot to death, but there were no birds. In fact we hadn't heard so much as a gull since arriving. The cooler air felt heavenly, but tempered by the confirmation of no water source. I'd been hoping to hear it trickling from somewhere in the recesses, but there didn't seem to *be* recesses. We dared to venture slightly beyond the reach of the sun and the passageway narrowed considerably until we were practically walking on our knees.

We turned back. The cave would make a good shelter from a storm but we didn't care to linger. It smelled musty and its tight confines reminded me of jaws struggling to clamp down on us. We agreed to sleep on the beach instead.

"Someone will come," Grant said as we looked out at the ocean. "Someone has to."

But we could see for miles, and no one was coming.

5.

We slept the first night on the side we washed up, close to where we dropped our supplies. I should say we tried to sleep, but I never felt like I made it. The coolness of the night quickly lost its initial pleasantness, but Tanya showed no interest in huddling close for warmth.

Digging HELP in the sand was my idea and warmed us up in the dawn before the sun started bearing down. Tanya suggested we use rocks to spell it on top of the hill too. A passing plane might see it, but I was more hopeful someone would aim a satellite our way and do something about it if they saw our signs. If they zeroed in closer still, they might mistake Tanya's eye rolling for grand mal seizures. The long night hadn't softened her any and the feeling was mutual.

We waded out to catch fish but they apparently had better things to do than hang out near the mystery island because opportunities were few and far between. When we saw a stingray, we hauled ass to the beach. Grant threw a rock in its direction like a shotput which splashed only about twenty feet from the target.

"This close," I said, holding up thumb and index finger.

Grant flipped me off peeled banana style, which made me hungrier. You can guess how Tanya reacted.

Day two felt like six days, minimum. The smartphone wouldn't power on. If boredom were edible, we'd have been okay. Instead we sniped at each other for being thirsty and hungry, or rather I sniped at Tanya and Grant and they took turns sniping back as a tag team. We tried to distract ourselves, often making it worse. Grant asked what our desert island CDs would be, and they ganged up on me for saying, "I don't know, let me see what I grabbed off the boat before it sank."

"This is such bullshit," Grant said at another point. "We've got all this water out there—we never stop hearing it, for Christ's sake—and we can't drink any of it."

"We could," I said, "we'd just dehydrate faster from the salt."

"Dehydrating from drinking water." He laughed humorlessly. "Man, that's just not even fair."

"We'll probably have to drink our own urine after we run out of water."

Tanya had the face of a child hearing the urban legend where the babysitter discovers the calls are coming from inside the house.

"Don't listen to him," Grant said. "It won't come to that. Even if we don't get rescued right away, it won't matter. It'll rain."

We looked to the horizon where the sky was pure azure, not a single cloud in it, fluffy white or otherwise. If the ocean didn't ripple, you could almost confuse one for the other.

"It'll rain," Grant repeated. "It has to."

6.

It didn't rain, not the next day when we used up the last of our water, or the day after that. Plenty of clouds floated past but always wispy or as clean as snowfall. We named the shapes, but no one bothered forecasting rain from anything we saw. The skies darkened only for the arrival of the night, and I'd never seen the stars clearer in my life. Like I could have shattered them with a stone from the ground.

7.

"What about the tree?" Grant said on the second day with no water.

We were hiding out in the cave. I'd been playing sentry beneath said tree with the flare gun for unknown hours before this, having stretched my shirt and one borrowed from Grant out across two limbs to create some shade to sit there and watch for passing ships. There wasn't enough to comfortably shield two people so Tanya had a ready excuse to stay behind with Grant. We decided to stay on the side with the cave since it offered shelter from the sun, and we had a look-out to the other side with a little climb from the cave.

"I've been thinking about it too," Tanya said. She often seemed to have been thinking about the latest thing Grant said, funnily enough. I suspected she'd make the same claim if he'd said, "What about animal husbandry?" I also suspected they were fooling around, even though it would have been stupid of them with no fluids to spare. I could creep to the edge of the bluff and see what they were up to, but who knew what happened when they holed up in the cave. That's when I usually made it a point to clamber down for someone to take my place. We were deciding who should take next watch when Grant made his proposal.

"It's something, right?" He sounded excited, and he and Tanya both stood up.

"Yeah, we'll die if we don't try something. I've never been so thirsty in my life."

12

"Wait a minute." I followed them out because they weren't stopping for a dissenting voice.

The sun nearly melted my contrarian attitude by the time we attained the summit. It would have been easy to roll the dice and sip. If I didn't automatically hate everything Grant and Tanya agreed on, I might have caved.

"You don't know what's in that stuff," I said.

"We know we can drink it," Grant countered. "That's a better offer than the rest of the island is giving us. That's good enough for me."

"Me too," Tanya said. "Have some of your piss if you're too scared, Ben."

"At least my piss definitely isn't poisonous."

"Poisonous?" Grant laughed. "Dude, it's a tree, not a mushroom."

"There's poisonous sap."

"Ben, it's not poisonous, okay?" Tanya said.

"I guess we're about to know for sure."

They stood near the coated branch, the only one of the limbs with that slippery appearance. Tanya winced from the sickly odor of the ooze, something that kept me from giving its consumption serious consideration during the hours I watched from the ground, parched with thirst and stomach gurgling. It reminded me of disease for some reason, tempered my hunger with nausea.

"Here goes nothing." Little syrup stalactites depended from the underside and Grant knelt beneath them with his tongue out. A couple pooled on his tongue like motor oil until he drew it in and swallowed. "It's not good," he reported. "But beats dying of thirst any day."

Tanya guided her face below the branch for her first share. She clearly wanted to spit it back out but finally swallowed it down. When she licked the residue from her lips I thought of rubber cement.

I shook my head when they asked if I wanted in and they gave me disgusted looks, although less so than from the act of actually drinking the tree jizz a couple more times. It was enough for me that it was there as a last resort, like a cyanide capsule in a false tooth. I did drink my urine that morning before they got up—it almost looked orange—but it hadn't helped and I'd nearly thrown it back up because the aftertaste was wretched. The thirst was consuming me again, would have been all I could think about if not for Grant and Tanya, but I wouldn't trust my fate to the mystery ooze while I had the chance to see the effect it had on them, at least overnight. I could hold out that long.

I hoped.

"See?" Tanya gestured. "We're both fine."

"Yeah, man," Grant said. "You're depriving yourself for nothing. FYI, we're eating you if you drop dead."

I doubted they would cry themselves to sleep tonight over that so I didn't say anything, just walked back to the cave with them. I wondered how many more times I could do that without being so dizzy that I pitched over the side. Or how many more times I'd have the strength to make the climb in the first place.

8.

The sun had nearly emerged from the horizon as if borne of the water when I woke up and made sure Tanya and Grant were fortunately (I guess) still alive. They also hadn't spent the night doubled over puking or shitting their guts. I suppose I looked quite the fool for my protest, but I'd gotten comfortable with that role ever since accepting Grant's invitation with Tanya.

I examined them as they slept. Tanya was undeniably pretty, sunburns notwithstanding, and I didn't mind seeing so much of her ass and legs each day. I had a fantasy of her pulling her bikini bottom to the side, telling me to fuck her. That ship had sailed, though, or at least smashed itself to pieces and dropped to the ocean floor.

Grant, on the other hand—

"What the hell…"

A disgusting insect poked through one leg of his swimming trunks, something like a giant grub/millipede hybrid. The bulge ran all the way to where his package should have been. I didn't understand how he could sleep through that, and expected him to bolt upright amidst much falsetto shrieking. I seized a nearby stone with hopefully enough heft to smash the little bastard (the insect thing, not Grant) dead. I tapped the rock on the ground, hoping the thing would withdraw to investigate, but it didn't move.

My rock cast a shadow over the pillar of disgust. It had little rubbery fronds along the visible duration of its length, which looked greased up with something like pus, and had the thickness of a garden hose. It made me sick to look at it.

I tried once more to coax it away from Grant, tapping it through the fabric and nudging it in my direction.

"Ben, dude, the fuck?" Grant said.

So barely brushing the fabric of his trunks disturbed his sleep in the way some dick-sucking insect couldn't.

He sat up straight and scooted away, maybe thinking I was about to smash his junk. Instead of evicting the thing, it went with Grant even when he stood up. The tendril just hung there like a curtain cord.

"What?" Tanya rubbed her eyes, groaning as she strained upright.

I pointed. "Grant! In your shorts!"

He looked down and his eyes popped. He slapped at the thing like a lick of flame. I stood ready with the rock, ready to crush it as soon as it dropped off, but it didn't release.

Grant ceased his slapping almost as soon as he started. "Oh shit…oh Jesus." He collapsed on his ass in the sand, holding his head in his hands, chest hitching like he was working up to a scream.

"Is it…latched on?" I advanced with the rock.

He held up a hand. "Stay back! Don't touch it!"

Tanya stood beside me, wide awake now.

Rather than trying to yank the thing out, Grant pulled his trunks down below his waist so it would cover it up.

"You want the rock?" I prepared to pitch it to him, though he had plenty of alternates in reach.

"It's not latched on," he said, returning his hands to his head and shaking it miserably. "It's *me*. It's *me*." He kept repeating this as if it could help him integrate the madness with reality.

"Let me see!" Tanya took a step toward him and he drew up against the hill, burying his face in his arms, ordering us away. Ostrich syndrome with a side of millipede dick.

I shook off a twinge of jealousy. She didn't want to see it because it was his thing (which she'd probably already seen, sucked and fucked anyway). It was more like the morbid curiosity over a two-headed calf, but she wouldn't desire such a thing, even if that two-headed calf owned an island estate.

"Come on," I said, "let's give him some space."

As we walked away from him and the awkward sound of his crying—the real reason I wanted some distance—I couldn't help thinking, *The winner…by default…Ben!*

But there was no real joy involved. The ramifications were as hideous as they were impossible. The tree did that to Grant, and Tanya drank from it too.

I kept a hand on her back. "How do you feel?"

"I'm fine, really," she said, but she pulled her bikini bottoms out to check. I wasn't sure of the etiquette there so I looked to the ocean and tensed for her scream. It was hard to reconcile the beauty of the sun-dappled waters and the renewal of another day with Grant's mutation. The natural and the sickeningly unnatural.

"All clear," she said.

I turned back as she brushed away tears.

"Maybe it only has that effect with guys," I said.

"Maybe." The tears continued and I put my arm around her. I didn't believe for a minute she was out of the clear, and she didn't either. I was ready to pull away from her at the first sign of a change. I wondered if Grant still wanted us to be found.

Tanya stopped walking. "Not too far. We have to make sure he doesn't start digging into the first-aid kit."

"Why's that?"

"It has scissors."

9.

Grant volunteered to be the look-out, like nothing had happened. I wondered if he planned to throw himself off the top. I wasn't sure what to say. They didn't make a greeting card for genital transformation.

I went up with him to watch him per Tanya's request as well as to clean up the HELP sign on the other side while the sand was still shaded. The tide had eroded the crescent of our P. I was less concerned with some satellite-savvy grammar Nazi ignoring our plea to teach us a lesson than just getting away from Grant and letting him do what he thought he had to do.

Shade or not, the heat was still bad enough and I thought I was hallucinating when I looked up and saw Grant doing what he thought he had to do with his trunks around his ankles, thrusting with abandon into the tree as he hugged the trunk. The thrusts were disturbingly long with the added girth, so the mutation hadn't been all bad—he'd packed on those several extra inches which had allowed the new appendage to be visible beyond the hem of his trunks. He was the Johnny Wadd of biological abomination, for what that was worth.

He shuddered visibly and slumped against the tree for several seconds, and then like a child determined to learn to ride that bike without the training wheels, he started pumping away again at a different hole. The P was neat as you could please now and the furrows of the letters nice and symmetrical, but I wouldn't go back up until he'd returned to his post.

There was a lot of hip thrusting and spasms before he withdrew from the tree and planted himself back on the ground, shoulders hitching. A destroyer could have cruised by and he would have missed it. I began the hike back up the hill, convinced it was the last time. I wouldn't have the strength to do it again. It hit me that the sun could do its magical dance along the ripples of the ocean again two mornings from now and I could be rotting to a dry husk in the sand.

I was going to pretend to have missed all of Grant's sex show to avoid the awkwardness and keep the status quo.

"I can't stop fucking the tree," Grant said measuredly the second my shadow fell across him. "I'm about to get up and fuck it again. I can't stop, Ben. It won't let me."

I thought I'd maxed out at wanting to be anywhere else in the world before then, but it turned out there was still another level after all.

Grant continued. "Wants me to fill it up. I must. Soon. You were right. Never should have done it, Ben. Never should have drank the tree jizz."

Thankfully I at least had something to say now. "Pretty sure it's you shouldn't have *drunk* the tree jizz, man. Just sit tight and holler if a ship comes, okay?"

I noted that the ooze now hung from the underside of the limb for nearly three feet, stretching to within inches of the ground. Longer, thicker than before. I walked away fast as I dared. He'd resumed the tree vigil and begun grunting behind me at roughly the same time I heard Tanya's screams.

I found her in the cave, a writhing shape beyond the reach of the sun. I couldn't see her, only heard cries of horror and pain on my way down which sounded disturbingly less identifiable as human by the time I reached her. The heat and lightheadedness played spatial tricks where the darkness looked like a black train racing away from me endlessly, and a swarm of blue spots filled my eyes from the reduction in light. When she slumped into the path of the sun, I trusted my sight even less.

She had stripped off her shirt and her skin rippled all over, as if it had taken a liquid form. I thought of the golden specks of sunlight this morning from a marginally saner time. She had swollen all over like a puffer fish, half again her size.

Tanya held her hand out to me as protrusions undulated through her arm, some moving toward her hands, others to her shoulders, while a couple more spiraled around the limb. I thought she tried to say *help,* but she'd been reduced to choking sounds.

I might have been screaming that whole time too, as it seems like I'd already begun before the burrowers started to emerge from Tanya's mouth. They had a similar appearance to the thing Grant had been sticking into the tree, but this was a colony of them, pouring from her gaping mouth like raw meat through a grinder in a mass exodus, and the crank kept churning them out in an unbroken stream. Hundreds of them, maybe thousands. And not just her mouth either, as others sought a more immediate exit than the long line for the oral aperture. They pushed through her eyes, nudging them aside to spill from the sockets. They left a snail trail in their wake upon flesh and stone, the same pus-like discharge as Grant's mutation. Her bikini bottom bulged as a ball of them erupted from between her legs. She had to have died before this but her mouth kept working as the burrowers emerged, giving her the awful illusion of life and sustained horror through prolonged parasitic vomitus.

If they'd shown any interest in me I would have run straight through the mouth of the cave into nothingness for the fastest way down and away from them, but they had a hive mind mentality that guided them into the recesses of the cave. To nestle, to breed?

Tanya lay slack and withered, draped in an ill-fitting skin that seemed partially melted without the buoyancy of those slimy things.

Melted.

My loathing for them, both what they did to Tanya and their sickening existence, pushed me to fire the flare gun after them when it seemed like they had all evacuated their incubator. The corridor exploded into piercing light as the flare sizzled until the cave narrowed and it struck a shelf of overhead rock. The extent of the progression turned my empty stomach, this lubricated moving carpet pouring down a black gullet. The flare reigned upon the congregation in blistering fragments, and their putrid coating did nothing to stave off the ignition. A large swath of them went up like dry grass in a brush fire and spread the same, illuminating the full extent of the cave.

We'd assumed it led to nothing or that it wasn't large enough to provide us access if it did. We didn't bother exploring because we had no light anyway, but now I saw that it didn't narrow so much that we couldn't have crawled all the way—a mere fifteen yards or so—and what seemed to be a barrier at the end wasn't after all. Flaming burrowers poured through it and vanished beyond.

I reloaded the flare gun with a cartridge from the case and jammed it behind the waist of my trunks, and followed while some stragglers allowed me the light to reach the end. The floor was wet and sticky beneath my palms and knees, sometimes bubbling as I maneuvered around scorched remnants. I prayed for no open wounds.

The other side promised more light as the burrowers continued to burn. The barrier was wet and malleable, like touching a giant eyeball. I winced as I wormed my way through its slit, thinking of a rubbery coin pouch.

I only wanted to ensure the incineration of the whole colony, or to fire another flare if need be. I'd hoped they'd do me the convenience of a central location, but I forgot all about that as I beheld the other side of the orifice.

The recesses I'd originally hoped for were here, but not as a network of tunnels with a fresh water source. The ground beneath me had the same membranous texture as the entrance and the color of human gums. Above me were organic structures, as massive as allowed by the structure of the hill. One looked like bubble wrap made of flesh and sinew. I saw pulsing sacs bigger than me. The burrowers had been crawling toward a pair of enlarged egg-shaped sacs and had kindly congregated in their death throes to sustain my light source. An enormous structure of tubes, twice my size, hung at the edge of the illumination. They looked to be tied in an impenetrable knot. Maybe it was a trick of the light, but I thought I saw them moving like a tangle of serpents.

The hill was more than what hung above us, though. The moist ground beneath me eventually terminated in a ridge, perhaps leading to more organs, tissues, sacs, and systems below.

Wherever we'd landed, it was alive. I didn't know if the rock, sand, and tree were part of it or something it became part of, the way its secretions had made those changes in Grant and Tanya. Maybe it was marooned too and adapted us as Tanya and Grant tried to adapt to it. Its needs were as unknown to us as its existence, but they seemed unmistakably procreative. If it succeeded, I thought dehydration was probably the best case scenario for me.

I fired the flare. I aimed at the bubble wrap structure nearest to me overhead. For all I knew the whole cavity could have gone up like a kitchen with a gas leak but it didn't happen that way. A wave of heat engulfed me as it lit up, and one of the nearby egg-shaped sacs caught as I was deciding if I should reload. I thought I'd hear some kind of deafening shriek but there was nothing.

I crawled back through the oval and on through the cave. I still hadn't ruled out an explosion but I had only fumes left in my reserves, and a tortoise would have blown me off the race track. The susurrus of the ocean continued to call me until I made it past Tanya and out the opening. The waves seemed choppier as if some maelstrom simmered below. Behind me a spark of light remained, like the watchful eye of some creature way back in the darkness.

11.

Grant hasn't returned. I'm waiting for the strength to drag myself back up the hill. There's one flare left. I think I can get him and the tree with the last shot if he's still stuck in his feedback loop of trunk or treat. I have to. I don't think he'll be Grant much longer, and I don't know what could happen if he worked up a thirst right there next to his preferred sap.

Then I need to make it down to the ocean to wash the residue of the cave from me. I think I'll be doing well to make it to the top, though, and getting down under my own power will be the stuff of miracles. But I wonder if I do make it down there what I would see if the current took me away until I sank like a stone to the depths, the great unknown on the underside of the island.

Garrote
Lydian Faust

I'll bet you never even heard her sing. My Mya. Voice of an angel, but her screams were Satan shooting fire up my spine. Did you at least hear Mya scream? Naw, you were probably quick with the wire. A little scared of getting your ass kicked by a girl, maybe? She wasn't really even a girl to you anyhow, was she? Just another "feminazi." You could tell by the uniform, couldn't you? Sure you noticed I'm dressed like Mya was that day, down by the river. Ripped jeans tucked into combat boots, ratty covert tee, flannel tied around the waist, studded leather jacket. It was chilly that night, after her show. It's even colder now. I imagine you can see your breath. Won't look behind me to verify. You're close enough now that I can hear you without straining. You're still relatively new to this. Mya was only your fourth, right? Ah, here you come, boy. Getting louder now. Still nowhere near as loud as you were on those

BROCHAN boards, mrkeyboardwarrior69. Serial killers are supposed to be smarter than this.

BROCHAN
mrkeyboardwarrior69: dispatched another dyke today

gihulkdik: nice bro. need more soldiers like u on the front lines

yeahyoutoo: u fuck her first?

droogdrugthug: please tell me u gave her the ole in-out-in-out

beastafphil: how big were them tits dude? some got big titties under all that baggy shit

mrkeyboardwarrior69: shit no. ugly af. choked her ass out & threw that trash in the river

mrkeyboardwarrior69: looked like a dude and I ain't no fag

yeahyoutoo: ain't no fag either but chicks here ain't puttin out. take what I can get

bossbearfightR: rich dude like mrkbw69 ain't got poontang probs tho

mrkeyboardwarrior69: loaded. no probs wit tha puss. speaking of- duty calls. L8R assholes

You're close enough to smell now, mrkeyboardwarrior69. Reeking of CKOne. Quite an androgynous choice of fragrance for someone so very masculine. The manliest. Hands strong enough to kill a bear, or punch a shark, or wrap around some dyke's neck and choke her out. Except you don't use your bare hands. You prefer the garrote. Why? Don't you want to touch that warm, tender skin? Feel the pulse speed in panic, then slow, then stop? Love that rhythm. A proper end to a song. Not sure you're the musical type. Think I can change that.

mrkeyboardwarrior69 felt sick every time he logged out of the BROCHAN boards. He wasn't anything like those losers. Didn't live in his mom's basement. Wasn't some canned-cheese smelling fatty, pasty from gaming 24/7. They disgusted him but were the only ones who could come close to understanding him. This last BROCHAN session left him not only sick but frustrated. He was filthy fucking rich. Should have women clawing each other's eyes out to ride his fat dick. He had a pool no one swam in. A chalet but no Swiss miss. Beachfront mansion in Nassau but no Bahama mama. Hell, he'd settle for dating that chubby brunette who worked at the GAP at this point. Just wanted pussy he didn't have to pay cash for once in a while. Hookers made him wanna puke. Diseased cunts. When he had tried to chat up the GAP chick, he'd stumbled over his words and she just wrinkled her nose and silently handed him his bag of khakis. He never was good with words.

Numbers were something he was good with—very good. Quadrupled his trust in the market in five years. His folks, had they been around, might have been impressed. He hoped they were having a good time in Belize or wherever the fuck they were hiding these days. He actually couldn't give a shit. Mom and Dad's front-page newsworthy money-laundering scheme had left them ostracized by their fellow elites. Rachel dumped him. Friends iced him. His parents fled the U.S. days before his eighteenth birthday. Left him with a soon-to-be-seized mini palace and two stupid poodles in sunny SoCal. He got a belated birthday card a few weeks later with a Panama postage mark letting him know they were alive and to take good care of the fucking poodles. He dropped the poodles off at the pound and moved himself up to Seattle.

Thank fuck for the trust fund gramps had left him. Feds couldn't take his money. He was untouchable. He gazed at his bronzed naked visage in the mirror and did a few more reps on the Bowflex.

I am a rich God. Every bitch will be mine. Even the lesbos. Especially the dykes.

As mrkeyboardwarrior69 did a few more aggressive leg pumps, he thought about getting some more action down by the river that night, and his ego grew by a few centimeters.

Sharper than I expected, your wire hugs my throat. Frustrated by my lack of response, you double down. No smack-talk? Disappointing. You didn't say anything to my Mya as you choked the last breath out of her? My sweet songbird died in silence? Probably for the best. I'll bet your voice is shit. Common shit. We'll see, soon enough. Ah, applying max pressure now. Tantrums. Silly boy with a string. It tickles. Can't help giggling.

"What the--? Are you fucking laughing, you stupid bitch?"

Tears of laughter streaming down my cheeks. You pull the garrote as tight as you can and press your semifreddo log into my thigh- trying to dive the point home, missing by several inches.

"Why the fuck won't you die, cunt?"

My chest clangs from giggling so hard. I gasp a bit before responding.

"Put the toy away now, Gabriel."

"What? Bitch, how the fuck do you know--"

"Prefer Gabe, then? Or should we be more formal, mrkeyboardwarrior69?"

You fumble with the garrote. Snatching it from my neck, I throw it towards the water's edge. Sinks like a silver snake in the grassy bank. I'm an admittedly shitty poet. Centuries of wasted attempts.

"Gabe, know it sounds funny, but I really do like the pain. Mya, though, she didn't like the pain, did she?"

Your blue eyes wide, you stumble away from lil ol' me.

"Who the fuck is Mya?"

You look like you're going to run, so I soften my face and clutch my ruby talons to my chest, where the heart would be.

26

"My Mya? You mean you didn't even know her name?"

"I don't know who the fuck you're talking about, you psycho bitch!"

You puff up, a little bullfrog. I raise my palm in peace.

"Mya was a singer. And the best screamer I'd ever heard. Was going to have her join me as a second vocalist for my band. Was going to make her that offer the night you followed her from her show and murdered her in this very spot. You remember now? She looked a lot like me. Did you even get to hear her scream?"

You size me up, weigh your options. Flex your measly home-gym muscles and decide you're going to have fun fucking with my weird ass. Abnormally strong, but probably just another crazy ho on snow, you figure. Anything to preserve your fragile ego.

"Scream? Ha! Dyke didn't make a peep when I snuffed her ugly ass, thank fuck. Caught part of her show, actually. Sounded like a dying cat. Don't know why anyone likes that shit. Not real music- just a bunch of lesbos in boots yellin' about how held down they are. Bullshit. Her voice sucked. Did the world a favor, taking that bitch out."

A throat punch effectively silenced you, and the doused handkerchief pressed to your fat mouth put you down for the count. I'd like to pretend that I usually use more sophisticated methods, mrkeyboardwarrior69, but the truth is I love a bit of the ole ultra-violence.

mrkeyboardwarrior69/Gabe hazily awoke on a blue velvet chaise and looked up to see a circle of scowling faces. The closest belonged to a statuesque ebony god with silver dreads dangling over Gabe's mouth. The man smacked his cheek, sent spittle flying, marring the velvet.

"Get up!"

Gabriel Mercado hadn't responded so quickly to a command in his entire posh life. He'd never before obeyed *any* command. Gabe was a silver-spoon suckled prince. If he wailed for cake, his parents bought him a bakery.

27

'Sweets for my sweet,' his mother would say, leaving Gabe to his gluttony whilst she went to get hammered at one of her endless charity luncheons. She made him toaster-strudels in the toaster-oven a few days a week, just to validify her stay-at-home mom status. Those were his favorite mornings. And sometimes his least favorite, when his Dad joined them for breakfast and bitched about the lack of Denver omelets, his mom's fat ass, and why the hell they were paying a cook if his mom kept giving her days off. Pans were banged, coffeepots shattered against the wall, and why the fuck did all of his hamsters keep dying?

"What the hell have you dragged in now, Selene?"

Santi's massive hands pulled Gabe up by his blonde-tipped hair to leer at him before roughly dropping him back onto the chaise.

"Gentle! Don't ruin the merchandise, Santi!"

"Merchandise?" Santi chuffed, poking Gabe with his black claw.

"You remember that singer I wanted? Mya?"

Selene's bandmates, Santi, Francisco, and Morgana nodded.

"Well, I couldn't get Mya because this walking specimen of human excrement got to her first. Got his hands on her before I could. Didn't use his hands though, the fucking coward. Used a wire. A garrote. Murdered my angel."

Santi hocked a gob of phlegm at Gabe's forehead and boomed with laughter as the kid frantically rubbed it off.

"You're telling me this pathetic piece of shit's a killer, Selene? Well, that's fucking hilarious, but what the hell did you drag him here for?"

"Yeah, he's not your usual taste, Selene," Francisco snickered, ruffling his bony fingers through Gabe's stiff hair.

Selene nearly gagged at the suggestion.

"He's not a snack, Fran. mrkeyboardwarrior69 here is our new backup singer. Well, backup screamer, that is."

Morgana, the drummer, rolled her eyes.

"Don't want this panty-waste in my band. No fucking way."

Gabe cleared his bruised throat and spit a bit of blood before ejecting, "Yeah, let me go! I'm not a singer, for fuck's sake!"

Selene sauntered over and casually smoked him in the temple, knocking him out. She smiled, with teeth. Her bandmates knew that smile. There'd be no stopping Selene.

"Guys, c'mon! We can whip him into shape! This jack-ass is gonna be a perfect addition to the album!"

No one protested this time. They did love a project.

mrkeyboardwarrior69 slept like a shark, his eyelids held open with guitar picks (Francisco's homage to his favorite Kubrick flick). When Gabe's pupils finally rolled back down, they focused on Selene, the grinning demon, floating inches from his face. Tried to close his eyes. Was met with searing pain. Opened his mouth to howl, but no sound escaped.

"Oh, sorry, you're on mute."

Selene laughed, waving a remote across his field of vision.

"Don't worry, you'll be getting plenty of use out of that voice box. It's steel. Built to last."

Gabe writhed beneath his straps in agony.

"Suffering, my little fuck-boy?"

Selene gestured up towards the recording booth window and music swarmed Gabe's brain. Music only he could hear. Double bass drum. Sloppily speeding licks in drop-D, and, unexpectedly, the sweetest voice he'd ever heard. Sarcastic and saccharine.

"Beautiful, isn't it?" Selene floated down to his pelvis and tapped his prick to life. Arousal made him painfully aware of something wrapped tightly around his penis. The picks dug into his eyelids as he tried to shut them against the pain and his lips curled back against his teeth.

Delighted by Gabe's reaction, Selene stroked his crotch.

"Feeling that now, are you? Those are high-E strings, wrapped around that teensy cock of yours. Think of it as a choke-chain. Stay in line, lil doggie, don't struggle."

With a wink, Selene jerked her thumb up at her band-mates, gleefully watching behind the glass. The angelic voice in Gabe's head grew twice as loud, inducing a nausea all the more dreadful because no bile could rise from his metallic gut.

"My Mya had the most exquisite voice. People made themselves sick over her voice. Know you'd never heard it, but listen to her now. Love it, don't you? Would you've killed her, had you heard her sing? Mya sang for every one of God's misfortunate creatures, myself included. Wanted so desperately to have her join our merry band of monsters. You took that chance from her. Can you feel the pain in her voice?"

Immobile, Gabe stared at the ceiling, wondering why his pried eyes hadn't already dried out. Mya's honey-warm voice filled one ear, while Selene's words ice-picked the other.

"Well, can you feel it?"

Gabe remained still.

With a press of a button on Selene's remote, the high-E strings wrapped around Gabe's penis pulled tautly, in opposing directions. Not enough to sever. Just a choke-chain.

"Two more beats of the song and you'll feel it. With our dirty blood now in your veins, you'll feel it forever. And with your stainless organ modifications, you'll have little need to feed. Future just keeps getting brighter for our kind! Ah, one, two, three, here it comes, your vocal debut."

Selene nodded at the window. Santi pressed record.

Sound engulfed him. Mya's tinkling voice growing up, getting stronger, gaining gravel, building into a primal scream that tore through his guts up into his heart.

Selene unmuted him.

If the sound of spattering blood were a song, it would have been Gabe's searing cries. Selene heard a #1 single in their future. Santi, a neuroscientist, reveled in his accomplishments. Thanks to his modifications, every one of Mya's recorded screams triggered a pain response to Gabe's parietal lobe.

Morgana, the drummer, grabbed Francisco's frigid paw and pulled it towards her breasts, pressing her pert nose against the glass- a kid on Christmas morning.

"Watch my part," Morgana giggled, squeezing Fran's thigh.

Mya's recorded screams stopped. So did Gabe's.

Following that nanosecond pause, a slow, off-time, deliberate beat crept between Gabe's ears. Building up heavier. Faster. FASTER. Over the music in his brain, Gabe couldn't hear the mechanical whirr of the arm unfolding from the table beneath his spread, strapped thighs.

"Here it comes, you sick fuck," Morgana whispered.

A beat as heavy as Mya's corpse dropped hell into his brain. Simultaneously, a naked kick-drum mallet smashed onto his testicles, bursting them like putrid grapes. Morgana, the former engineer, still had it in her. She squealed and bit Fran's plump lip. Santi raised his ruby glass to them and they clinked.

"Cheers! To the band."

"Cheers!"

"Cheers, Santi!"

"Forever!"

It warmed Selene's decommissioned heart to see the band bonding again. Meanwhile, Gabe's screams were legendary, even in L.A. Her merry band of misfortunate robot-vampires toured that year, en masque, under the moniker GARROTE. Gabe's backing vocal screams were quite popular in the BROCHAN community. Selene made sure to regularly upload new GARROTE tracks to the forum from Gabe's account. She even posted a pic of her claw stroking mrkeyboardwarrior69's string-choked dick. Bros ate it up. Selene considered keeping him around for a sophomore release. In memory of Mya.

The Junkyard Shift
Ryan C. Thomas

Harry is an outdated name, even for a thirty-two year old. Which is why I don't think Harry's name is really Harry. He looks like a Wayland, or maybe an Adam, but not a Harry. But I don't want to ask. I'm sure he'd tell me his real name if he wanted to, but nobody I work with wants to tell me anything real about themselves; it's the nature of the business. No names, no real friendships.

Storage facilitators, that's why they call us. Bunch of young, able-bodied dudes slinging bags of flesh in the hot Texas sun. Must be 101 degrees most days, and the flesh smells like twice-regurgitated rat shit. I use Vicks under my nose and wrap a bandana across my face, but goddam that smell cuts through it like a chainsaw through cheese.

I watch Harry grab a black trash bag from the back of the panel truck. It's bulbous, like usual, and a bubbled pocket in the very bottom speaks of a collection of noxious liquids that would make even the most hardened criminal puke. He drops the bag on the once-blue tarp.

"Heavy one," he says. His voice is muffled through his own bandana, a black one that sports a skeleton's lower jaw. He wipes an arm across his forehead and leaves a streak of brick red over his eyebrows. He already has other red streaks near his temples, but these are dried and flaky from the heat, stitched with tiny cracks like the salt pans of Death Valley. His black t-shirt is wet with sweat and his jeans are torn at the knees.

"Just one bag today," he says. "Thank Christ we won't be here all night like usual."

"What's it to you, Harry," I say, "thought the girls on your street work late anyway."

"Fuck you, man. I don't pick up that street trash no more. I get paid good for this job. I hire the good stuff. Top shelf pussy, you know what I'm saying?"

I know Harry has a predilection for hookers. He told me he killed one of them recently. Said the girl wouldn't lick his asshole so he choked her right there in the hotel. Said watching her eyes pop near out of her head made him cum on the spot. I'd asked him if he was scared her pimp might come after him. He just laughed and said he was ready for it. But thankfully for him this job affords him some protection from that kind of low lever street crime. Chances are he's safe. Our allegiance to this company comes with perks, one of which is we are off limits to non-affiliated street thugs.

Harry rips opens the trash bag. A collection of severed heads roll out onto the blue tarp, leaving trails of red and gray slime. Bits of pink goo slide down their waxen faces and spread out like runny pudding beneath them. A couple are missing their ears. One has had its eyeballs pushed into the skull. Another has tell-tale blisters from a butane torch. They are all men, the youngest a teenager, the oldest a white haired man with deep lines in is cheeks. Despite the varying signs of torture, they all carry the same expression

—mouths open, tongues lolling out, eyelids half closed, the pupils dry and buried beneath blood clots.

I stare at them like I always do, with wonder and disgust. Wonder at the biology of the human body, with its bones and sinew, blood and flapping skin. Disgust at the sight of maggots squirming into nostrils, of flies lighting on chapped, dry lips before wandering into the gaping mouths, like spelunkers in a cave, eventually making buzzing sounds deep down in the throats. A few come out the other side, where the machetes have hacked through the vocal cords and thick arteries of the enemies of my employer.

"These fuckers stink," Harry says. He already has a shovel in his hands and begins pushing the heads into the pit we've dug in the back acre of this junkyard. They roll together as a group, the teeth smacking into one another with the sound of billiard balls connecting. I keep my eyes on the young teen, his blond hair coated with dirt and dry blood. He has three ink dots near his eye, most likely done by one of his friends with a guitar string in juvie hall. La Vida Loca. This crazy life. His head lands on the top of the pile in the pit.

"Ah, there he is," says Harry. He reaches down with his gardening gloves on, grabs the head of the teen and tosses it into the dirt near my feet. "That's the one you need."

"You got the paper?" I ask.

"Here." He hands me a folded piece of notebook paper. I open it and see an address. A part of the city we all know too well.

At my feet the dead teen's head is looking up at me. One front tooth is dangling loose, about to fall out. The cheek has deep slash marks on it. This kid was a fighter. But he wasn't strong enough. They never are.

"Hey, watch this!" Harry is undoing his pants. He drops them to his knees and sticks his ass over the pit, using the shovel as a crutch. He beings to groan, his face scrunched. I smell it before I see it, a spray of diarrhea as red as the dried blood covering the severed heads. It shoots out of his ass with the sounds of someone stirring Jell-O, filling the eyes and mouths of the dead. The flies go crazy. More food for their fiesta.

"That's the carne asada burrito from Aibertos," Harry laughs, shuffling away to the pick-up truck, some red watery shit running down the backs of his knees. He takes a paper towel roll and wet naps from the front seat and cleans up, tosses the waste paper in the pit. He hocks up a loogie and spits it in the pit for good measure. Satisfied with his irreverent act, he begins tossing dirt on them.

"C'mon, man, help me out."

"You should see a doctor, Harry. Your shit has blood in it."

"That's just the hot sauce coming out. Get that other shovel and start slinging dirt."

I'd like to tell him he's wrong, but it's not my place. Still, I know blood when I see it. Could be rectal cancer or could just be he enjoys anal sex when no one is looking. Lots of guys who do time in prison come out with a new affinity for anal play. I don't judge. Do what you want. You only get one life. Trust me, I know. Either way, that wasn't hot sauce.

I scoop up a mound of dirt and toss it on the collection of heads. It covers their mouths, then their eyes, then soon enough all the heads are buried. The stench of decaying flesh still singes the air but I know it will be gone soon enough. We've buried the heads several feet down, too far down for the coyotes to get at. For good measure, Harry grabs one of the empty oil drums from the back of the truck. He places it on the new grave, opens the top and starts filling it with dirt. It takes a few minutes to fill, creating a massive weight on top of the grave. No one will know what's buried here.

I grab the teenage head at my feet, noticing that dirt has stuck to the dead eyes. Even though this person is dead, it still makes my own eyes itch. I re-wrap the head in the trash bag, and toss it in the passenger side footwell of the truck. "Can you drop me off at home?" I ask.

Harry checks his watch. "Yeah, hurry up, I gotta be somewhere in an hour."

"So you do have a hot date?"

"Nah, told my kid I'd take him to the movies. He wants to see that new superhero shit. Frogman or whatever it's called."

"I heard it's pretty good. Breaking all sort of records."

"Better be good. I could be getting my dick sucked instead. But a father's got a responsibility, right?"

He jumps behind the wheel and we slowly steer our way out past the junked cars, mounds of rusted appliances and piles of bent metallic detritus. All this crap once meant something to someone. Now it's forgotten, lost to time.

The severed head is heavy in the duffle bag as I walk down the street, watching kids play on the stoops of the low-income housing units walling me in on both sides. I've got my gloves on, my head down in a hoodie. In a nice neighborhood I'd be suspect, but here I just blend in. The day's heat rises from the blacktop, along with the stench of garbage and dog shit. I know the moon is above me somewhere but it's masked by smog and light pollution from the nearby oil refineries.

I check the address on the paper Harry gave me, look up at the crumbling four-story walk-up to my right. This is the place. I watch a rat scurry around the steps to the entrance. It grabs a crumb of something and disappears into the shadows. This is poverty. This is why I work, to not be here.

When I enter the building, I hear televisions and hip hop music coming from the units. Someone down the hall shouts about something, and there is a loud bang on a wall. People are pissed. The heat will do that to you. Poverty as well.

The unit I'm looking for is on the third floor, and so I trudge up the steps looking at the gang tags on the handrails. It's all kiddy shit, nothing to be afraid of. These kids don't know real gangs, not like I do.

The head in the bag swings against my legs as I climb. I can smell the flesh rotting. The scent rises up the stairs with me. Copper, meat, decay, dirt, urine, it's all there. You never really get used to it, you just learn to deal with it. I'm not wearing my bandana; it would be too conspicuous. I still have remnants of the Vicks under my nose, but it has worn off and isn't really helping. The stench turns my stomach if I get too big a whiff, so I keep my head turned away.

I hit the third floor landing and move down the dark hallway. I hear pots and pans clanging behind the doors, more TVs, someone singing. I find the unit halfway down and set the bag on the floor. I put my head to the door, listen for sounds from within. I hear nothing. I use the lock pick set from my pocket to undo the deadbolt. I wait for the interior security chain to catch but it's not there. Either it was broken off or never installed. Probably the latter. Saves me the trouble of having to break it myself.

The apartment is dark and smells like onions. A dark couch is in front of me, a handful of clothing over the arms like someone was doing laundry. I see streetlights through the faded curtains at the end of the room. It's enough light to guide me to the kitchen, which is just to my left.

"Home again, home again, jiggity jig," I say, unzipping the bag. I set it on the ground and remove the head. Even in the dim light I can see the half-closed eyes, still bloodshot, staring at me. "You picked the wrong line of work," I say.

I open the fridge and move a couple dishes around, some meatloaf and a casserole of sorts. It looks delicious, but I already ate before I came. Besides, I'm not here to rob anyone.

I set the head down in the middle of the fridge, just as my boss expects me to do. The lips have started to peel back from the teeth and the blood around the nose is almost completely dark brown now. A bit of neck bone fits nicely in the grooves of the fridge rack, keeping it from lolling sideways.

I hear a noise behind me, whirl to find an older woman standing there with a knife in her hand. She's in a bathrobe, slippers on her feet. Before I can say anything I watch a small child, perhaps five or six, poke her head out from behind the robe. A tiny hand grips her mother's leg, squeezing for reassurance.

"Who are you? What do you want?" the mother asks.

"Nothing," I say. "I was just leaving." I step cautiously toward her, staring her down, my fists clenched, letting her know that if she moves that knife toward me she will regret it. She moves around me, visibly shaking, one hand on her child, letting me pass. Finally she sees the head in the fridge and screams. The sound is a klaxon in a submarine, and though I know it will go unnoticed for a few minutes in this impoverished hellhole, eventually it is sure to draw neighbors.

The child starts crying. The mother falls to her knees in front of the fridge, reaching for the head but not touching it. "Manny! Manny!" she cries. "Not my Manny!"

I reach the front door, notice the family photo hanging on the wall. Manny, his mother, his little sister, and a father (I assume) who is nowhere in the apartment. Manny is smiling, his blond hair clean and gelled. His face free of blood and decay. He looks like a happy teen. They all look happy.

I open the door and step out into the hallway.

"But why!?" she cries out behind me.

I don't owe her an explanation, but for the sake of the little one I say, "I expect it's a message to your husband. Or you. I dunno. I just do the deliveries."

"Why!" she screams again.

I think about this for a second, then add, "Because if you're gonna live this crazy life, make sure you understand the hazards." With this I shut the door and leave, listening to her cries, and the sobs of her small child, all the way down the stairs.

Outside again, duffle bag in hand, the kids are still playing on the stoops and the rats are still running in the shadows. I walk the ten blocks back to my car, passing empty parking lots behind chainlink fences crawling with weeds. In the shadows I see all sorts of vagabonds and gangbangers. They all leave me alone. Perhaps they know me, perhaps they don't.

I come upon a bus stop where a couple of police officers are questioning a hooker. I see my car at the end of the street, waiting for me. I'm tired and I just want to drive home to a better neighborhood than this. It's been a long day.

"What are you looking at?" the nearest cop asks me.

"Nothing."

"What are you doing out here?"

"Just coming home from work."

He looks me up and down. "This late?"

"Yeah."

"Sounds like a shitty job."

I smile. "It's a living," I say, and head to my car.

Cougars
Michelle Garza & Melissa Lason

The taxi reeked of alcohol and sweat. Three young Americans sat crammed against each other in the back seat. Rusty's head bobbled as the car navigated the winding roads of the mountains outside of the small Mexican town. His friends on each side of him hadn't imbibed in the local tequila as heavily as Rusty, and their excitement hung like static electricity in the confines of the shady cab. The driver didn't speak any English as far as they could tell but had been instructed to take them to a place where they could find the company of the wildest women in Mexico. At least that's what the bartender promised them at the cantina in the red light district.

"I need me somethin' exotic!" Rusty slurred, looking to Brandon and David.

"That's what the guy promised, girls that knew how to really get us off."

"He said older women, experts in pleasure." David reminded him.

"Fuck yeah, I love me a cougar!" Brandon said and dug in his pocket to find his flask.

Rusty held out his hand but Brandon refused, "You're already toasted, if you're not careful your jimmy ain't gonna work."

"What the fuck are you talkin' about? I've never had whiskey dick!"

"Sure!" David said and chuckled as Brandon handed him the flask, ignoring Rusty's outstretched hand.

The driver lit a cheap cigar and turned on the windshield wipers as rain began to pelt the taxi. It rounded a corner and continued to climb into the rugged mountain range. Rusty remembered looking out the window of his hotel room, staring at them, thinking the hills looked like a painting hung in the sky, they were so far in the distance. Hours later he climbed into a faded yellow cab, and now his destination was those very mountains.

"We're lucky we weren't kicked out after your little stunt." David said, looking at Brandon.

"What? Are you still mad about that?"

"I thought that bartender was going to shoot you, ya jackass!" Rusty said.

"Those girls get paid to be felt up, how could she suddenly have morals?" Brandon asked and laughed.

"You don't get to check their oil for free, asshole."

"It wasn't free, I made it rain all over the stage." Brandon protested.

"A bunch of one dollar bills," David said, "look out for Mr Moneybags!"

"Shut the fuck up," Brandon's voice rose. The taxi driver glared at him in the rear view mirror and he grew quiet before finishing his sentence, "we come down here to have the freedom to do whatever we want. The locals know how it is."

"Yeah, they look at us like we're all fuckin cavemen like you." Rusty said.

"Whatever, she was just young and stuck up. The older ones don't mind a finger up the ass." Brandon said and hit the flask.

"The last time I had an older women it was my mom's new neighbor." Rusty boasted nostalgically.

"No way, that redhead?" Brandon asked.

"That's her!"

"How was she? She looked like a fox!"

"Kinda boring. I was hoping she'd really tear me up but she didn't."

"Not every older woman is a cougar," David said, "only the ones who really get freaky. The others are just, well, old."

The three chuckled and continued to sip from the flask. The driver glanced into the rearview mirror, and a smile slid across his face as he whispered something to himself. The passengers never heard him over the battering rain.

The taxi came to a stop before a mansion shrouded by the eaves of ancient trees.

"Look at this swanky shit!" Rusty said.

"This is a true brothel, like the ones from back in the day." Brandon spoke in awe of the palatial estate tucked away in the mountains.

The driver stuck his hand out the window, waiting to be paid.

"You wanna come in with us, old man. Maybe be our translator?" David asked.

"You won't need one." A voice answered from the dark.

A dark haired woman came down the front steps. She was dressed in red, her black hair hanging down on her tan shoulders like ebony silk.

The driver grabbed the handful of cash David held. The old man took three of the bills then wadded the rest up and threw it out the window as he sped away.

"What's his problem?" Rusty asked.

"He has work to do, and he has to leave a cut for knowing our location, it's a well-guarded secret." The woman answered. "Won't you come in and make yourselves comfortable?" She asked, her smile inviting.

"Lead the way, Darlin'," Rusty said.

She turned with a wink and they watched her strut back up the stairs. The way she moved her hips drew them along quickly behind her as she made her way to the large wooden doors of the entrance.

"Welcome to La Casa Del Gato."

"Is that the cat house?" Brandon asked. His Spanish didn't extend beyond his high school classes but he felt confident in his translation.

"Very good." She complimented and pushed the doors open.

They stepped into the expansive bottom floor. The walls were painted a deep maroon, the furniture upholstered in black velvet. There was a fireplace and a long, dark wood bar set with crystal glasses and a multitude of different types of liquor. There were a dozen naked women lounging on the velvet seats and lain out across plush couches, just waiting for the American men.

"This is paradise!" Rusty said.

"I'm not sure if we can afford this." Brandon whispered to David.

"Don't worry," the mistress of the house spoke as she closed the door behind them, "I'm sure we can accommodate you."

She clapped her hands together and the women assembled before the vacationers.

"My name is Mistress Felina, have your pick of my girls and they'll take you upstairs."

"To be honest," Rusty spoke, "We're looking for some cougars, ya know, older women."

"I assure you they look younger than they are, they have ages of experience." She answered with a sly wink.

"Why don't we all have a couple drinks first?" Rusty suggested.

"Sure, make yourselves at home." Felina answered.

The naked women surrounded them, carrying bottles of liquor and fine crystal glasses to them. They caressed the three young tourists and kissed them softly on the lips.

"I don't think I can hold out very long." David said.

"Take your pick of the girls, more than one if you like." Felina spoke, filling a glass of champagne for herself.

Rusty pointed to two women who both had black hair and the same delicate facial features. They resembled each other so much he wondered if they were twins. "I'll have me some of that."

"Very nice choice," Felina said but held up her finger and pointed it at him, "just remember to be a gentleman, too many come from the north and act like my girls are animals."

"I'll treat them like queens." He smiled, swaying slightly from the effects of the booze.

Brandon was being led by three women towards the staircase. He didn't protest as they had already started stripping his clothes from his body.

"What about you, Miss Felina?" David asked. "Are you on the menu?"

"If you think you can handle me." She giggled.

When she smiled he could tell she was older than she appeared but still in incredible shape.

"I bet I can." He answered, feeling his blood flush his cheeks and stiffen his cock.

"Follow me."

The three were taken to the second floor of the sprawling brothel and taken to grand bedrooms. House cats scurried in the corridors, their sleek fur felt like velvet against the young men's legs as they playfully zigzagged between their feet.

"Luckily I'm not allergic to pussy!" Rusty joked.

The women giggled but he wondered if they understood him at all. He didn't really mind as long as they comprehended when he asked them to spread their legs, or if they'd deep throat him.

He was shown to a bed with crimson sheets. He tore off his clothes and climbed onto the velvet blankets as the two women joined him. They were already nude, their tan skin was tight and flawless. He wiped his mouth, pretending to brush away the drool of his anticipation. One of the ladies went right to work by grabbing his stiffening penis and teasingly lapping at it. He sighed and laughed when she meowed like a kitty cat. The other climbed over to him and ran her tongue up the side of his neck and started to nibble his earlobe. Her breath was hot as she panted with desire. Her breast rested against his arm, soft and supple. He began to think he had died and gone to heaven as she continued to kiss his neck then down his chest to nip at his nipple softly. She moved to hover over him and let her nipples graze his lips. He breathed deeply as his body reacted to the sensation, his heart raced and his dick throbbed with wanting. He wanted to make it last, get his money's worth, but the two women catering to his sexual fantasies were more than professional. They were magical in their knowledge of turning a man on.

"This won't last long if you keep doing that, ladies." He spoke.

He nearly cried out as the meowing prostitute took him deep into her mouth. He could hear moans from another room, his partners clearly getting the royal treatment as well. He grabbed the back of her hair as she slid him in and out of her mouth slowly and deeply. The other girl straddled his chest and playfully squeezed her ample breasts and ran her hands down to her shaven cunt.

"Sit on my face." He whispered, pointing up to his tongue as he licked his lips.

Again he worried she wouldn't understand but she gently crawled into position over his mouth. He stuck his tongue out as she pulled her dainty labia apart. He could feel her quivering as he let his tongue explore her. She was wet already and horny. He wondered how long it had been since they had any business, the two seemed as though they really needed some dick. She excitedly began to move her hips. His own pleasure was skyrocketing at the masterful way the second girl sucked him. He felt her pull him out of her mouth for a moment and the bed shifting as she got ready to ride him. Warm and slippery she slid down onto him, letting him feel every inch of her from the inside. He paused in his licking at a tickle of a hair in his throat. He felt a surge of embarrassment but he nearly gagged and internally cursed both the prostitute's shave job and the house cats roaming the establishment. A commotion from a room across the hall broke his concentration. The girl above his face fell down, nearly smothering him. In confusion he reached up and gripped her hips. They were covered in hair. Moans from the other room were now screams, not of pleasure but of terror. With all of his strength he tossed his lover from him and coughed as he opened his eyes to see what rode his dick now in ferocious movements was no longer the beautiful Latina who led him upstairs. It was a beast, covered in thick black fur, its ears jutted out from the top of its head. He put his hands on her chest to try to push her off his deflating erection but she was strong. Her face appeared human yet also very feline; her golden eyes stared at him hungrily. The beast meowed, a guttural mockery of how a cat actually sounded, then slashed his chest open with razor-like claws attached to the ends of her elongated fingers. The second woman came into view. She too had changed into some kind of cat from hell. He realized what was stuck in his throat, the fur of the cougar riding his face. He coughed and vomit rose in his throat. The brothel was filled with horrified cries that died in moments to be replaced by the meows of countless cats, both of the natural variety and those vile beings that lived between human and feline form.

"You Americans are all talk, have been for centuries. You wanted older women, here we are." A voice hissed from the doorway.

Rusty turned his face to see an upright cat creature. In one hand she held the heads of his friends by the hair. She cackled as cats came swarming from the hallway, winding between her monstrous feet, meowing hungrily.

"No! Please!" He begged. "Please!"

"I thought you big, tough, American men could handle a little pussy?" Felina teased.

The cat beasts forced him down onto the mattress, their gaze fixed on his naked flesh. He recognized the emotion in their eyes now; it was not from being sex starved, it was from being ravenously hungry. They fell onto him, all teeth and claws, slicing him open. Helpless agony filled him as it dawned on him that no one knew where they were, that no one would come to free him from the cat house.

"What's the matter? I thought you liked cougars?" Her laughter was monstrous and was punctuated by unimaginable pain as the two cougars tore into his stomach. A flood of cats leapt onto the bed to join their humanoid sisters as they fed.

Guinea Pig Blues
Chad Lutzke

My dogs sniffed out the infection right away, stuck their head right into his lap. They knew. Me? It took visual cues to catch on. Despite the smell.

I hadn't seen Nate in over a decade. We shook hands and I offered a seat on the patio in the shade. The reunion called for beer, so I brought out the best and we wasted no time in popping caps. I was excited to share my newfound love for writing with my old friend, but the conversation quickly turned to economics and the cost of living. There was a lot to bitch about.

"It's not just here, you know. They're gouging the price of gas all across the state. Back in the day I could fill that same tank for a fraction of the price." Nate pointed toward the driveway where his Honda Civic sat in a rusted heap. A stark contrast against the flowers my wife had planted earlier in the year that lined the drive. "Hell, I wouldn't have had half the fun back then if shit was the way it is now. We'd all be broke."

"I wouldn't call selling bunk weed to follow The Dead fun, but to each his own," I said, and got a chuckle out of Nate.

"Hey, you do what you gotta do, man."

"Yup. That's why I still run the record store. I don't make shit, but she's still open."

Nate shifted in his seat, tugged at his cargo shorts. He must have put on eighty pounds since I'd seen him last. Neither of us mentioned it. If you'll pardon the pun, it was an elephant in the room.

"That surprises me, what with the kids streaming their music nowadays," Nate said.

"Fortunately for me the hipsters like their vinyl. And of course you've got your old-school collectors. They're few and far between, but they're around."

I found a window to bring up my writing, to share with my old friend the news about my first published article. A piece I wrote in just a matter of an hour at the computer and was compensated well for. The publication gave me the writing bug and I was flirting with the idea of closing my store altogether to take up writing. A dream I'd always had but never pursued.

But that's when the wife came out, and with her the dogs; and the dogs took to Nate right away. Not to his chubby, back-scratching fingers but to his crotch. They stuffed their faces between his legs like there was a biscuit buried in there. This was no ordinary, uninvited crotch sniff. This was magnetic and unnerving. The hair on their spines stood up, tails halted their usual guest-greeting wags, and there was a low growl too, muffled by Nate's meaty thighs and drooping pannus.

Shocked by my dogs' reactions—or was it their dedication—I didn't say a word. I watched.

"Get!" Nate yelled. "Get outta there!" He slammed his legs shut and the dogs yipped. Their tails went from rigid to limp and tucked as they scurried away toward my wife.

"I'm so sorry," she said, embarrassed—for him or for herself, maybe both.

Nate tugged at his shorts, smoothed them out, pressing them with a careful caress of each leg. I swayed the attention elsewhere. "Honey, you remember my old roommate, Nate."

An immediate *yes, of course* would have helped the tension, but instead her response hung as she looked him over, noticing the weight gain, the thinned wispy hair.

"You've grown a beard!" she said. A redeeming save.

Nate tugged at his shorts once more and stood to greet my wife. The effort was laborious.

"Good to see you, Kathryn." They shook hands. I was fixed on Nate and the way in which he stood. He was careful in his movement, something I earlier attributed to his obesity. But it was more than that. Something was off.

"It's been what, ten, eleven years?" my wife asked.

"Closer to fourteen. I was selling cars at the time, saw your husband wandering around the lot. The two of you had just gotten married."

"It's been that long?"

Nate held his legs close together like a child needing to pee. And then a trickle of liquid crept down his leg and into his sandal—opaque yellow with the consistency of milk. He hadn't even felt it. Or if he did, it went ignored.

My wife took the dogs back inside and told Nate not to go anywhere because she had banana bread in the oven and insisted he have some. He told her he'd be happy to, then sat back down. The patio chair cushion shot air from all sides and with it a pungent odor I knew had come from him. I was smelling what had drawn the dogs. Rotting chicken, spoiled cheese. It was repulsive.

"You got yourself a keeper there, buddy," Nate said.

"I sure do," my tone dead and distracted.

"And what is she doing these days?"

"She's a psychiatrist, got her own practice over on Columbia."

"No shit? Well, someone's gotta bring home the bacon."

It stung, but it was true. The record store hadn't been doing nearly as well as I'd led on. The hipsters, while they grew fond of vinyl, liked their Amazon and their eBay. My store, it seemed, was strictly for the wandering collector looking for hidden gems, all too often never finding them.

"Well, I do have a plan B I've been working on."

"Yeah? What's that?" Nate opened his legs, then closed them as though subtly adjusting himself like men do on hot summer days. The smell lingered.

"I'm thinking of becoming a writer."

Nate gave me a moment like he was waiting for a punchline, then laughed. "A writer? Like Stephen King?"

"Not really. I haven't written much fiction, but I did recently sell a piece to a magazine."

"Really? Which magazine?"

I was hesitant in telling him. His tone was condescending. I regretted saying anything at all.

"Reader's Digest."

Nate laughed again, a little too hard.

"I don't know what you're laughing at. I got two hundred bucks for it."

"I thought only housewives wrote that shit."

"Well, now you know better."

"I just don't see you as a writer, man...I mean, congratulations on the fluke sale I guess, but I don't know that I'd bet the farm on a career from it."

It was at this point I recalled the hell of being room-mates with the man. The belittling, the pessimism, the unwillingness to ever work more than he had to. If there was a way to sit on your ass and get paid, Nate would find it.

With impeccable timing, my wife came outside with a tray of banana bread, two more beers, and the mail—a letter addressed to me from the nation's leading music magazine.

"I think you've been waiting for this, dear," she said, excitedly.

I had. It was a response to a lengthy article I'd submitted through the post. An article on the downfall of independent record stores and where the industry may be headed based on the observations of one small shop owner.

I stared at the envelope while Nate dug into the bread. The letter was either ammunition for his pessimistic outlook or a slap to his smug face. A well-needed one.

"Well, what is it?" Nate asked, a mouthful of food.

"Just a letter. I'll open it later."

The wife gave me a look. I gave one back, and I think she understood. I also think she could smell the presence of something unnatural between Nate's legs. Her lip was curled with subtle disgust and I could see the questions wanting to spill, to ask what in God's name was that intrusive odor. But she kept quiet and went inside, her cheeks puffed in a contained gag.

Flies had begun to congregate on Nate's foot where the leak had seeped. How he didn't feel them, I'm unsure. Habituation?

"If it's important, don't let me stop you," he said.

I told him it was no big deal, that I could wait. I couldn't bring myself to be rejected in front of the one person who never invested an ounce of faith in me. Yes, it all came back. Every bit of cynicism and arrogance he still hadn't lost.

"So, what is it *you've* been doing for work these days?" I fought back.

Nate squirmed in his seat, adjusted himself again, adding a fresh cloud of stink to the humid air.

"Oh, you know...a little bit of this, a little bit of that. Overall you could call me a scientist of sorts." He didn't look at me when he said it. It sounded like bullshit. "I don't suppose you've heard of Johnston Study Corp?"

"Nope."

"Didn't think so. They're over in Baton, an independently funded research lab, mostly biological research, the link between man and animal, plant and man."

I got the feeling he was trying to intellectualize his role at the lab, inflate his importance. He'd done this plenty when we were roommates. His only job ever—being a guinea pig for Upstart Pharmaceuticals, where he'd stay for a weekend and be monitored while being fed blood pressure medication—or sugar pills for placebo—for three days and walk out with $400, or $1200 if he stayed the entire week. To the uneducated—mostly the occasional girl he'd meet—his role was bloated to that of a "scientist." The lie smelled familiar.

"Scientist huh? I didn't realize you'd gone back to school."

Nate chewed on the bread much longer than needed before answering, buying time.

"I didn't. Just like you didn't when you wrote that article for the woman's mag. Think of me as a free-lance laboratory technician."

"You mean guinea pig."

I'd struck a nerve. His face wore the weight of a frown, a lying child confronted, elbow deep in the cookie jar. He took a swig of his beer and helped himself to another piece of bread, ignoring my remark. Or thinking of a way around it. While the reason for our lengthy hiatus from one another was apparent to me, Nate didn't recognize the confrontational man before him. The pushover was gone - that scrawny, pimple-faced kid with little self-esteem.

"We all do what we've gotta do, man. You sell records, I use what the good Lord gave me."

"If you put it that way, then I suppose I did the same when I sold my first piece, used what God gave me. My talent."

"Talent? It's a mag for old folks and stay-at-home moms. When you're selling to Rolling Stone or Time then come talk to me about talent. Until then I wouldn't go around bragging."

I glanced at the envelope sitting on the tray next to me. I wanted to open it, to prove I had what it took, but I feared he was right. What if the article I'd sold *was* a fluke? What if I never sold another piece again? I'd continue selling vinyl to has-been hippies dipped in patchouli and old school, graying anarchists looking for Misfits first pressings. A dead-end job with a head full of dying dreams.

"Okay, Nate. What is it you're researching exactly? What are your scientific skills rendering? How are you bettering society with your biological prowess? Let's hear it. Please, proselytise."

Nate swallowed his bread, sipped his beer. "Antibiotics. More specifically the use of biological means to rid the body of disease. It's a homeopath's wet dream, our research. Johnston's is trying to do away with unnecessary pharmaceuticals with the hopes of not only sustaining life but upping the quality of it."

"And your role is?"

"I'm not a guinea pig. I'm...a vessel. And I provide valuable data."

It was like a garbage man telling you he's the overseer of waste management, an exporter of antiquities.

And then Nate scratched his leg, his shorts hiked up, and I saw what was unmistakably a large, black leech attached to his yellowing leg, sucking from a chaotic display of red and blue webbing under his skin—a blood-filled map of rivers and freeways on jaundice terrain.

I drew my eyes away with the image burned in my mind, a lingering haunt until later when I'd see worse. The alcohol was in full effect and nearly gave me the gumption to intrude, to ask what in hell had he done. But somehow, even in my inebriated state, I was frightened by the sight, the odor. I just wanted him gone and to run inside with my letter and be rejected in solitude, where my wife would offer continued support and encouragement. Instead, she showed up with shots of tequila complete with lemon slices and the salt shaker.

Then things got ugly.

Nate spotted the drinks with hungry eyes. "Oh, you don't mess around, Kathryn. I don't think I've had tequila since your hubby and I celebrated the approval of his loan to open the store. Remember that, Bill?"

I remembered it. I hadn't offered, but the tab was on me. Including the hooker Nate found himself with later that night.

"I do remember that, and here we are a decade plus later and I'm still buying the drinks." My tone was matter of fact, devoid of humor. There was nothing funny about Nate and his lackadaisical lifestyle, his mooching, his desperate and disgusting ways of staying afloat.

My wife looked at me with a smirk. I think she liked the confrontational side of me. Something she didn't see often. Nate, on the other hand merely brushed the statement off, wriggling in his seat with a crotch full of pestilence, ignoring the obvious need for medical attention.

"Same 'ole Billy Walren, can't just be happy that someone's there to share the bottle with."

I caught Kathryn rolling her eyes as she headed back inside. It was time to ask Nate about his health, about the obvious—the rotting of his groin, either by aid of the giant leeches, or more than likely the cause. It could no longer be ignored. But before I got a chance, Nate spilled a generous amount of salt onto the back of his hand and raised the shot of tequila.

"To science...and to dreams that never come."

"And to those that do," I said, raising my own.

Nate found my own toast humorous and licked his hand clean of salt, a grin parting his face. He didn't even make it to the tequila before clutching his large stomach— the fleshy lid that covered his goods, hidden away from even himself. I pictured them blue and red and yellow like the inside of his thigh, perhaps worse.

And that's when the foaming started.

The leech I'd seen earlier fell to the patio and writhed around on the cement—a little vampire left in the sunlight. It reminded me of hooking a healthy worm, going every which way and wondering what just rammed up its ass. Or through its face.

But it wasn't the critter dropping out that flushed Nate's face red. It was the yellow-white froth that spilled from his shorts as he struggled to keep his shit together while shifting in his seat, moaning like a twin-filled woman in labor. And I'll admit to some morbid satisfaction at the sight, seeing his twisted experiment—the wise scientist— fail and reveal itself in a most disgusting and embarrassing manner. I was even tempted to crack a joke regarding the inability to hold his liquor.

As he stood, more leeches fell, squirming in agony. He tried collecting them, scooping even the curdling fluid back into his pants as though it may go unnoticed if only he acted quick enough.

Nate grunted and groaned as the years of lazy alternatives caught up with him. The smell was unbearable and I launched my own bodily fluids atop the growing puddle below him, beer and banana bread mingled with the pus and dark, glistening parasites as they wriggled in the purulence like spastic children in a mud-filled kiddie pool. And as I involuntarily bent to lurch yet again, another leech dropped and splashed in the putrid stew. But this one held with it a souvenir from its temporary home between Nate's legs—a shriveled patch of skin littered with kinked black hair. Nate's empty scrotum. It sat in the mess like the shell of a gourd, a baked potato split and

57

scooped empty. And then I hurled once more. Nate ran for the patio steps, his legs covered in genital viscera, and a single testicle bounced free against the steps, still attached by fleshy twine—a plum-shaped fetus, its umbilical cord still intact.

While Nate ran screaming, running from the terror that was his lower half, I leaned against the house and collected myself, wiping my chin and catching my breath. Nate plowed through the flowers and entered his car, backing out before his door was even shut, then it slammed and he raced down the road, the plum-fetus dragging in the street and behind the car like horrific newlywed decor announcing the passengers inside had just gotten married, until it finally broke free and rested in the street, waiting for oncoming traffic to pop free the contents inside.

Kathryn stood behind the screen door, her hand on her mouth. "I'll get a mop." She said, then disappeared.

The leeches lay curled and stiff like the oversized shavings from a child's black crayon. I sat back down, lightheaded and dizzy. The letter sat next to me, asking to be opened. I complied and tore at it with sadistic intent, unfolded the paper inside. Wrapped by the letter was a check for $375. For just a moment, I wanted Nate to come back—like a dog to his vomit.

The grin on my face spread wide with bile-coated teeth as I ran inside and to my office.

I had some writing to do.

Blood on the Walls
Saul Bailey

10th March 1969

  As he took it into his mouth, Nixon was presently surprised by both the softness and flavour of J.Edgar Hoover's penis. The old cocksucker had obviously bathed, thought Nixon, as he explored the other man's helmet with his tongue. There was a hint of coconut, with a faint pungency underneath, and the skin was smooth, silken. He felt the old queen shift beside him, and the warmth around his own cock increased as Hoover took him deeper inside, grunting slightly. Nixon felt his body respond to Hoover's mouth, growing tighter. Nixon closed his eyes and tried to think of Pat, imagine it was her mouth on him, as he often did in the shower, when he would masturbate furiously into the curtain bearing the presidential seal.

  Those sessions, so satisfying in those first weeks of January, had already begun to pale, and by early March, he'd suffered several unsuccessful attempts when Hoover had mentioned The Ritual. Nixon had resisted at first, suspecting some kind of elaborate hazing, but a part of him had found itself yearning for any kind of physical human contact, even from someone as vile as J Edgar. So he'd abandoned his efforts at self-pollution, and now he found himself glad of it, as he felt his cock start to tingle and throb in the mouth of the more experienced man.

Hoover grunted twice, indicating that Nixon needed to work harder. All right for you, thought Nixon, you've had the practice. Probably get your cock sucked three times a day. Still, the importance of synchronicity had been impressed upon him forcefully, and he made himself take Hoover's penis deeper into his mouth.

The effort brought Nixon's face closer to Hoover's body, and the smell was less pleasant. Nixon felt his belly turn a little, and his own cock become less rigid, his orgasm retreating. Fuck! Nixon screwed his eyes shut tighter, trying to ignore the smells in his nostrils, the taste in his throat, tried instead to concentrate on the skilled mouth and tongue working his cock, tried to picture Pat's mouth, those pouty lips, sliding up and down him.

Hoover grunted once, and began to thrust. Nixon was shocked, and nearly gagged as the head of Hoover's cock pushed deeper into his mouth, almost reaching his throat. At the same time, he felt his own cock respond to the moment, suddenly throbbing hard, twitching, beginning to pulse. He started to suck harder, pulling Hoover's throbbing cock into his mouth, and when it started to spurt in time with his own orgasm, he almost forgot not to swallow.

Later, as he brushed his teeth for the fourth time that evening, his gums raw and bleeding with the vigour of his attention, he recalled again the desire that had flooded through him as Hoover had begun to take his mouth aggressively, and felt the stirring in his shorts. But then he remembered the look in Hoover's eyes as they'd spat as one into the strange chalice the old queer had brought with him, and his cock wilted, his balls shriveling up protectively.

"He promised me a second term. That's all I want." He told his reflection, before flashing the old Nixon grin, just for practice.

His bloodstained teeth looked yellow under the harsh bathroom lights.

29th October, 2016
The smell was back.

Tom sighed and rubbed his eyes, frustrated by the tiredness he was feeling. His usual pattern was to sleep, uninterrupted and with no memory of dreaming, between 10pm and 5:45am, when he would wake, exercise and shower. This had been his routine since the Academy, and in the five years since his graduation. Chicago to California to Dallas to his current DC office assignment, the regime had kept him awake, alert, and stimulant free, unlike the caffeine junkies he was surrounded by on a daily basis.

But last night…he turned it over again in his mind, the absurd sexual ritual, with himself as Richard Nixon, the vivid nature of the dream, it's sights and smells…

He shuddered at the memory. No wonder he'd lain awake until gone 3am, unable to return to sleep, to his increasing frustration. He felt that anger rise again, now, as he struggled to focus on the screen in front of him. His eyes watered with the effort.

"Yo, Woody!"

Tom's head bobbed up, taking in the slouched form of Agent Parker in the doorway. Even though his suit was pressed, shirt clean, and tie on straight (but loosely knotted, the top button of his shirt peeking insolently over the top, not against regulation, but it made Tom's blood boil just the same), there was something dishevelled, even grubby, about Agent Parker, Tom thought. Something about his posture, the way he always leaned against the wall as a crooked angle. It irritated Tom at the best of times. This morning, coupled with his use of Tom's hated nickname (given by Parker the day they arrived in DC together two months ago, Tom from Dallas, Parker from Delaware - part of Parker's continued attempt to bond, despite Tom's cold rebuttals) and the chirpy tone, he felt a surge of rage so strong he had to grit his teeth.

"…yet?"

"Sorry, Agent Parker?"

"I said, you seen the memo yet?"

Tom's eye flicked back to the screen. His cursor was hovering over the first news item of the day, helpfully labelled on the bulletin board system: 'READ THIS FIRST!'. Carefully he unclenched his jaw and exhaled.

"Not yet, no."

"Wow, really? You're normally all over that shit. You feeling okay?"

Tom blinked a couple of times, to disguise the twitch in his left eye. He felt a small, needling pain starting to form behind it, the way it sometimes did when he was struggling with a tough investigation. His anger crested, but he would not allow it to break.

"I had a bad night's sleep. What's up?"

Tom pushed hard for a casual tone, hoping to move the conversation along, and he was relieved when Parker continued.

"The boss is reopening the Clinton investigation."

There was a pause, then Parker laughed. "I know, crazy shit, right? I thought it was a practical joke or something at first. Or maybe Anonymous had hacked the internal BBS or something. But no, it's legit, it'll be all over the media any second."

Tom shook his head gently, trying to push his chaotic, exhausted mind into coherence. His normally compliant and speedy thought processes felt sluggish, vague. He dragged his thoughts over to process, procedure.

"So standard media protocol?"

"Right, straight to media relations, strict 'no comments' to everyone - friend or foe, under pain of... well, pain."

"Got it. Anything else?"

Parker cocked his head, a slight frown drawing his eyebrows down.

"Did you want a coffee? I'm heading over to the pot." He waggled his mug in Tom's direction.

Tom felt a surge of disgust at the thought. "No, thanks." he said, attention already returning to the screen, opening the bulletin.

"Okay, suit yourself. Dunno what the hell Comey is playing at, though. I mean, we're eleven days out…"

"Mmm." Tom pretended to read the words on the screen, hand tightening around the mouse.

"Well. Anyway. Back to work."

"See you." As Tom heard Parker walk away, he willed his hand to relax, hearing the plastic of the mouse creak a little as he reduced the pressure. He closed his eyes and forced himself to breathe deeply. Just a bad night's sleep, that was all. A stupid nightmare. And that moron Parker winding him up with his inane banter.

And the smell. That God-awful smell.

He'd first noticed the smell at the field office in Chicago, six months after he'd been assigned. Then, as now, Tom had a distant, cordial relationship with his co-workers, so he'd had no occasion to raise it with them; no safe conversational gambit that might shake loose if it was a shared experience, or some bizarre hallucination. At first, he'd felt sure the others could smell it too. Something about their facial expressions, the distracted and stilted conversations, especially on the ground floor, where the smell was strongest. But as the days went on, these symptoms abated, until the office was once more functional, professional.

Then, after two weeks, the smell was gone.

The same pattern occurred eighteen months later, after a large transfer of newly trained agents were brought in - the smell, the initial reactions amongst the newcomers that suggested discomfort, gradually tapering back to normality, then an abrupt absence one morning, the air suddenly untainted again.

On his third year as an FBI agent, he'd been transferred to California, and within a week or so, the smell had arrived again. Like it had followed him. Tom began to have concerns that it was some kind of morbid symptom, perhaps of stress or a brain tumor, but he told no-one and sought no help and again, after a couple of weeks the smell simply vanished, as though it had never been there.

Tom felt his stomach cramp, interrupting his reminiscence. He frowned. His bowel movements were as regular as his sleeping habits - once after lunch, with a small one before bed each day - but, perhaps out of sympathy with his sleep deprived mind, his guts were apparently now also in rebellion. Tom's frowned deeply as he contemplated if he should hold it in; reassert control over his body, and in the process perhaps regain his routine. But then another cramp, almost painful, drove him to his feet and into the restroom down the hall.

At first, Tom didn't realise what he was looking at on the back of the bathroom door - his mind was too preoccupied with his unwelcome, unscheduled movement to focus properly - but as the immediate pressure was released, he had time to take in his surroundings, and his eyes widened. The white plastic of the cubicle door was interrupted by dark red splodges, small circles. It was an unmistakable blood spatter. It wasn't a spray pattern, nothing arterial or crime scene reminiscent. It was more like droplets from a cut or nosebleed that had been splashed onto the wall. He watched as one of the heavier drops welled and then ran down the white formica. Then his eyes moved up to his suit jacket, hanging from the hook on the back of the door.

His scowl was thunderous as he gingerly lifted his jacket from the hook and turned it over, eyes scanning the lining for stains. Nothing. He'd been incredibly lucky, he realised. Still. Blood. All over the back of the cubicle door. His eyes narrowed. This wasn't right.

Urgent action needed to be taken.

13th December, 1969

Hoover stands in the centre of the pentagram. The candles at each point hiss and spit, the human tallow filling the air with dark, rich smoke. The fat runs down the ornate, floor standing iron candle holders, dripping into the chalices positioned under each one. It sizzles as the drops land in the blood, sending more fumes into the air. The combined effect is like standing in the centre of a snake pit.

"I spit on the blood of the fallen King." Hoover allows the man's face to fill his mind, then replaces it with the photos from the morgue, those bright eyes blank and dull. That sonorous voice, silenced. He feels a hard on start to form. Got you, you uppity commie bastard.

Hoover spits towards the first chalice. He's practiced this many times, and his aim is true, the saliva barely troubling the lip of the vessel at it splashes into the contents.

He turns to his left, and the next point of the pentagram, the next chalice. "I spit on the blood of the Moslem traitor." He reflects on how long he'd had to keep the blood on ice for the ritual. Again he spits, and again his aim is true.

He turns. "I spit on the blood of the unnamed woman, whose voice will never be heard." Spits.

Turn. "I spit on the blood of the would-be martyr." Spit.

Turn. Last one. He feels his pulse in his throat now, the smoke in the room drying his mouth, even as mucus clogs his sinuses. The pressure. He has to be precise. The ritual cannot be repeated. To fail now is to fail forever. And he cannot fail. Too much is at stake. The future of the Republic. He blinks and wipes away sweat from his forehead.

"I spit on the blood of the fallen brother, the never-future king." As he inhales to spit, something catches in the back of his throat, and he coughs once, explosively. He feels something large leave the back of his throat, and time appears to slow as adrenaline fills his system, panic setting his heart pounding. The phlegm arcs across the room, and it's clearly going to overshoot, and he feels crushing despair flood his insides, mortal terror snapping at its heels, and then he sees a smaller mass detach from the larger body of snot, and the droplet falls with eerie precision into the centre of the final chalice.

Hoover lets out a shuddery sigh of relief. He has been tested, and not found wanting. He kneels, and retrieves the plate and chalice from the floor directly in front of him. He looks first at the milky contents of the chalice, then the small grey cube on the plate. The final

communion. Issue from one president, matter from another. Flesh and
fluid. He shudders, recalling the smell of Nixon as he came in
Hoover's mouth. But this is the last step, and he will not be deterred.

"And through this degradation most holy, the Southern Strategy
will be made flesh. It shall be claim a form, a vessel, a name. As I
take this unholy sacrament, it will live, and it will deliver us from
socialism and all its evils'".

With that, he pops the grey lump into his mouth, then takes a
swig from the chalice. As he masticates, the cocktail of Nixon's
semen and his own mixing with the brain matter of Kennedy and his
own saliva, Hoover feels a bright point of light open in his forehead.
He falls into it, through it,

Tom awoke with a start, utterly discombobulated. He
blinked heavily, shook his head, and tried to focus his eyes
on the screen in front of him. It was filled with row after
row of upper case c's. He rubbed the side of his face,
feeling the marks of the keys on his cheeks, and for a
second was filled with a rage so strong that he could barely
breathe.

"You fell asleep?"

Tom felt his face flush, cheeks red hot, burning with
shame. Parker stood straight in the doorway, regarding
Tom calmly. Tom scrambled for something to say, but
simply couldn't order his thoughts enough to do so. The
vividness of the dream, coupled with the shock of his
awakening, had stunned him into silence. Also, his neck
ached where it had been resting at an awkward angle,
rendering the simple act of holding his head up straight
uncomfortable.

"We're all working hard. But there's no excuse for
that."

Fear now mingled with the shame. Tom had expected
some kind of joke, more or less barbed depending on
Parker's mood, but this flatly delivered statement
suggested something far more serious. The thought of
being reported for dereliction of duty set Tom's heart

pounding hard and fast, nausea swirling in his stomach. He opened his mouth, but again, could think of nothing to say, so he closed it again.

The silence unwound, Parker staring, Tom staring back, afraid to, but afraid to look away, the pressure building and building, and to Tom the distance between them felt to be twisting, flattening out, but also telescoping, like a tunnel was opening between the two of them, invisible, but distorting the atmosphere. Tom could feel his heart pounding in his chest. His throat was bone dry, the memory of the foul smelling smoke of his dream coating his windpipe.

After some intolerable length of time, Parker blinked. "Here." He walked over to the desk and placed an object on Tom's desk. Tom allowed his gaze to move down to the FBI mug, three quarters filled with a black fluid. The rich, burnt smell brought the nausea on even stronger, and Tom flicked his eyes back up to Parker's face.

"Drink it."

Tom swallowed, heard a dry click. "I will. Thanks." The thought of doing so horrified him, and he had no intention of breaking the habit of a lifetime by allowing stimulants to pass his lips, but he realized there was little he wouldn't say at this point, to keep the matter of his falling asleep off of his record. Tom tried a smile, hoping it would show gratitude. It felt painful on his face.

Parker didn't smile back. He just stared. Close up, Tom could see how immaculately close his shave was, how neat and straight his collar and tie were. He had a smell to him, too - some mild cologne, or perfumed soap, but there was also something underneath, wasn't there? Tom thought so. Something faint, disguised, but oddly familiar. He could feel his tired, shocked mind trying to process, trying to bring something into focus, but the pain of his own smile was distracting him, frozen on his face, and the lack of response from Parker drew his attention back to the other man's face, his eyes. Again the silence between the two men stretched out, Tom feeling more frantic with each second, expecting some kind of laugh, or grimace, from Parker - some sign of that cocky, lazy attitude that was ordinarily so infuriating.

But there was nothing, His face was blank, neutral. Staring back.

Had a minute passed? Surely not. But it felt like it, all of it and more, a minute of silent regard, each second slower and more tortuous than the last. Discomfort had given way to fear, and fear was slowly blooming into a kind of terror, as Tom's tired mind scrabbled for purchase, trying to make sense of what was happening, find a way out of this silent confrontation.

He wants to see you drink.

The thought bubbled up into Tom's mind, arriving with a quiet insistence. He tried to push it away, to scoff at the absurdity, but it would not be denied. Surely not. Surely… But why else was Parker stood there, so close to his desk, staring at him with those blank eyes? Tom held the moment, and then reached slowly for the cup. Was there a flicker of recognition there, some tiny micro emotion on Parker's face, in his body language? Tom couldn't be sure, but he thought so. He felt the muscles in his shoulders clench, and sweat popped on his back.

He forced his hand to move forward and grip the handle of the cup, eyes rooted on Parker the whole time. As his fingers curled around the handle, he noted a small but definite shift in the other man's body language, a slight but perceptible drawing back. It felt like a gesture of approval, a sign that all may yet be well, but it was far from a full standing down or turning away, and Tom realized he would have to go through with it, all the way.

The smell of the coffee suddenly seemed overwhelming, and he felt his gut clench in rebellion. He despised hot and warm drinks of all persuasions, always had - couldn't even stomach drinking water at room temperature. But the impassive mask of Parker brooked no compromise. As he took in the other man, Tom was seized by a wave of hatred so powerful and unexpected that he had to grip the mug tightly to keep from flinging it in the other man's face.

The hatred was scary, terrifying even, but also enormously clarifying; in some strange way, calming. Tom understood, all at once, that he was locked in a scorpion dance with the other man - this moment, this confrontation, was a mortal one - that Parker had started a war which only one of them would survive.

Tom vowed in that moment that it would be him.

The vow gave him the strength to lift the cup to his lips. The distance to travel felt enormous, the cup implausibly heavy, but Tom completed the movement in one smooth action, not breaking eye contact as he did so. He pressed the lip of the cup between his lips, and tipped it towards him. He felt the warm fluid lap against the skin of his upper lip, and the acrid smell filled his nostrils. His mouth responded by filling with saliva, and he swallowed it carefully, keeping his mouth closed, before replacing the cup on the table, wiping his top lip with his free hand as he did so.

Parker immediately took a step back, body language relaxing. Tom no longer felt any need or desire to fake another smile. He took no pleasure in his tactical victory. He only wanted the other man gone, so he could plan how best to proceed. Tom made another vow; to never be caught on the back foot by Parker again. Never.

Parker nodded once, sharply. "You'll feel better soon", he said, then turned smoothly and left without a backwards glance. As he turned, Tom caught a glimpse of something on the tip of his right collar, but it was there and gone, and at the realisation that the other man was really leaving, Tom felt like a huge coiled spring in his midsection had been released all at once, and the breath left his body in a whoosh.

He wiped his face, lip snarling in disgust at his own perspiration, mind reeling. He replayed the confrontation, over and over, examining Parker's demeanor, so neat and tidy, unlike his normal scruffy self, his flat delivery, calm, unmoving face, the lack of aggression with which he delivered his demand, that neat tie and collar, so straight, so...

The smell of the coffee rolled up his nostrils, interrupting his thoughts, and suddenly Tom was struggling with a powerful urge to throw up.

He concentrated on his breathing, using a slow count of three before inhaling for three, holding it for three, and exhaling for three. He did it three more times. The nausea subsided, though he could feel it down there, a fire inside a deep dark cave. His mind slowly became calmer, though the stress of the confrontation and his own exhaustion meant his thoughts remained jagged, disorganized. Images flickered before his mind's eye - Parker's somehow neater hair, the way he'd walked into and out of the room, the knot of his tie suddenly snug against his white collar...

Tom's eyes widened, and his nostrils flared. *That's it!* The collar! He'd been distracted by the sudden surreal neatness of the tie knot, but there had been a single dark spot on the point of one collar.

Was that spot actually black, or dark red? Tom couldn't be sure, but he was, just the same. His mind returned to the toilet cubicle wall, and a small smile crossed his face.

Got you, you dirty blood flicker!

Tom took another three count breath cycle as he absorbed the new information. Clearly, this knowledge gave him an edge. Of course, Parker could still hurt him - falling asleep on duty, even in the office, was a very serious offence. But now Tom had something he could push back with.

The question was, how to let him know? He needed to send a message. *You hurt me, I hurt you. Back off.* He needed to...

Tom's eyes returned to his computer screen, and the small smile returned, unbidden and unnoticed, to his face. It would be anonymous, of course, but he would know, and he would know *he* knew.

Tom deleted the rows of extraneous C's, pages and pages of them falling before his highlight and delete, and completed the document. He read it through several times, then underlined two of the words for emphasis.

This was *it*. This would send the message. *Do NOT mess with me.*

He decided on a laminated print, and left his office to collect it.

The rest of the day passed uneventfully. Tom took advantage of his additional trip to the toilet to empty the coffee down the sink, but he retained the cup, placing it on the edge of his desk, and whilst the resulting lingering odor was unpleasant, it certainly kept sleep at bay. He had plenty of administrative jobs to get through, and the rhythm of that work was also comforting. Normalizing. Every time his mind drifted to the strange confrontation with Parker, he remembered his own response, and the thought satisfied him. They were now at an impasse, a Mexican standoff, but that wouldn't last. Parker was a slob. And sooner or later - sooner, was Tom's guess - he'd play right into Tom's hands.

All Tom had to do was stay efficient and alert, and act when the moment came.

"You didn't drink the coffee."

Tom froze, car keys in hand, momentarily too shocked to move. He'd been walking across the parking lot to his Prius, thinking of nothing but hitting the unlock button as soon as he was within the broadcast radius of the key. He'd made his usual 180 visual sweep of the lot, a habit so ingrained that he barely noticed it, but he'd not even thought to check if he was being followed. Tricky so and so must have matched his stride, followed him out the automatic doors.

Tom allowed his breath out slowly, turning as he did so. Parker stood before him, the same suddenly immaculate appearance and dead stare. That same tell-tale stain on his shirt collar. Tom kept his own face still, but inside, he smirked.

"You saw me, Parker. I'm really not in the mood for this."

Parker sighed - the first emotional display Tom had seen since he showed up with the cup of coffee and sudden demands that morning.

"Agent Wood, I think we should both go and see the boss."

Tom felt his pulse quicken, his mind rushing through the possibilities, trying to parse what was happening. Had Parker not seen the sign? Did he not know that Tom could hurt him too?

His eyes moved over Parker's face, looking for any sign of tension, or bluff. Nothing.

He doesn't know. He CAN'T know.

Tom weighed this information carefully, trying to game it out. They'd go to the chief's office, Parker would lay the charge… But what evidence did he have? Meanwhile, Tom could point to hard physical evidence to support his own claim of criminal damage to Federal Facilities - the dried bloodstain on Parker's collar. Lab work would verify the connection, if needed.

Tom had never lied to a superior officer in his life - indeed, before today, he would have found the very notion inconceivable. But as things stood, understanding the nature of his situation, and the mortal nature of his struggle with Parker, he realized with calm surprise that he was quite prepared to do so.

His mind went through this process on a single breath exhale. He inhaled, then said "Very well. Lead on."

He'd hoped to see some surprise at that, some flicker of concern, but Parker merely turned, impassively, and strode off. Tom followed.

Tom was led across the parking lot towards the small warehousing complex where the post and catering deliveries were made. He noted the lack of lights and activity, and reflexively checked his watch - 6:37pm. Late enough, he supposed, to explain why no-one seemed to be about. So why were there still lights on in one of the buildings - the only one with a huge semi still in the loading bay?

"This isn't the way to the chief's office." Tom was proud of how calm his voice sounded. He made sure to keep pace with the other man's swift stride, ensuring he was inside Parker's strike radius, eyes locked on the shoulders that would be the first part of his body to betray an aggressive move. Tom didn't think it likely he was going to be physically attacked... but after such a strange day, he was ruling nothing out.

As they approached the door to the bay, Tom realised the smell that had been bothering him all day - the smell that had seemed to haunt every field office he'd worked in at one time or another - was getting stronger with each step. He could feel it working at the back of his throat, tickling his sinuses, and he had to squint to stop his eyes from watering. Still, he maintained pace with Parker, determined not to let the other man gain a safe distance.

They reached the door to the warehouse. Tom was sure Parker would slow in order to open the door, and readied himself to stop, but Parker pushed the door open without breaking stride.

The smell hit Tom like a physical blow.

He fell to his knees and threw up, chunks of his mostly digested BLT on rye spattering onto the concrete. His eyes were screwed shut, tears rolling down his face, blood roaring in his ears. He barely felt the arms around his waist, lifting him.

"Shoulda drunk the coffee", Parker whispered in his ear, as he manhandled Tom, without any audible signs of effort, over the threshold and into the room.

"Open your eyes." The voice was low, grating. Like rust. Tom felt his stomach loosen, his bowels become watery. Fear chilled him, but in place of adrenaline, a lethal stillness, rigidity, sat in his muscles.

He didn't want to open his eyes.

He opened his eyes.

The light was cold. It spilled out from the open doors of the semi to Tom's left, and into the warehouse floor. In front of him, over a hundred people knelt on the concrete floor, naked, still and silent. Inside his icy calm, Tom observed the erect arm hair and stiff nipples, the goosebumps. The plumes of breath as the mass of people exhaled. They were the agents, the clerical pool, the cafeteria workers...though the light fell off, not quite reaching the rear wall, it seemed likely the entire field office staff was gathered here, naked and in supplication, breathing in the poisonous air with no reaction. They knelt in concentric semicircles around the back of the trailer. As Tom took in the scene, eyes still streaming from the caustic effect of the smell, he noticed with detachment that the entire back of the semi was a refrigerated unit that was running full blast, pouring cold air out into the warehouse.

"Come." The voice grated across Tom's ears. He didn't want to go.

He went.

His legs felt a long way away, barely attached, but they propelled him out along the side of the semi, and then turned him to face the open doors.

The inside of the container was dominated by a gigantic shadow. The shape was in front of whatever light source was at the back on the floor, so at first all Tom could make out was a monstrous black form, surrounded by a cold, almost blinding halo. The base was wide enough to fill the width of the space, and it slowly tapered up to a dome.

Tom stared into the darkness, trying to fight the tears in his eyes and the harsh backlight, straining to make sense of what he was seeing. His distracted mind reached for familiar comforts, and he held his breath for a count of three, then inhaled for three.

As he drew breath, something in the mass moved.

The effect was instantaneous. A wave of the smell hit Tom. His eyes felt like needles were being driven into them, and he screwed them shut. The pain also caused him to inhale more sharply, and he felt the lining of his throat burn as he took the foul air into his lungs. It was like being punched in the chest. He fell to his knees, screaming with pain. He tasted blood.

"Bring him to me."

Inside the darkness, his breath now damp and bitter, Tom felt hands, lifting him, propelling him forward. His skin began to itch, and he knew, with the intuition of mortal terror, that it was proximity to that misshapen, lumpen mass that his body was reacting to. He held his breath, heart thumping against his ribs, determined not to take any more of the toxin into his body.

No more. Not one more lungful.

Better to die.

"Your persistence is quite extraordinary. But it won't do, Agent Wood. It won't do at all."

Tom's teeth ground together. He couldn't afford to waste what was left in his lungs, so he did not cry out. The voice felt like worms, crawling into his ears, squirming in his brain.

"I sent you the dreams. And then I sent you the coffee. Why won't you drink?"

Tom could feel his heartbeat in his ears now, in his head. He couldn't hold his breath much longer. He could not let it go.

"Do you want to know how it ends?"

Tom shook his head, tears streaming down his cheeks, dripping from his chin.

He felt something touch his lips and...

He falls into the sky, until his beloved America is laid out beneath him, the bright lights twinkling like stars, the constellation of greatness, and then he rises towards the ground, a shooting star aimed at the east coast, New York, Manhattan, a tower, a room.

A young rich white man holds a voter registration form. It's been completed for him, with only the party affiliation blank. In his hand the tip of the gold pen hovers, uncertain. His brow creases. Hoover feels the magic flow into this kid, this fortunate son, and as it strikes his young mind, the spirit of the Southern Strategy nesting into his psyche like a tumor, the arm moves, and he places a crude x in the 'Republican' box. Then he laughs. "Who gives a shit, anyway?"

Blackness, then light. Hoover is back in his body, inside the pentagram.

The die is cast. The golem is set. The empire is secured. He should feel fulfilled. At peace.

And yet...

Something about the kid. His callous indifference. His facile joke. Yes, he's young - but this is the future. A great destiny.

The ritual worked. The spell was completed. Nothing can go wrong now.

And yet...

Hoovers mind turns to the other ritual. The one that can prolong a life beyond it's natural cycle. It's tricky. Painful. Requires great resource, cunning, and risk. It would take an enormous toll.

And yet...

Better safe than sorry.

Tom felt the tube pass his lips, enter his throat. It scraped the raw flesh there, and he felt blood start to trickle down his gullet, but he could no longer gag.

"Now, you will drink."

He'll destroy us all, thinks Tom, as he hears a gurgling noise, feels it rattling the tube as the fluid sloshes towards him. *The Orange King, he will end everything, he's out of control.*

"Yes. But he's still mine. Now drink."

Tom's mind was suddenly filled with an image, a vision - the other end of the tube in his throat, passing under the mound of flesh that was once a person, once the most powerful monster in the history of the Republic of the United States, into a rotting colon that is passing the fluid that will consume him.

He hears Hoover laugh. It is the last thing he hears.

The last thing he feels is something hot, pouring down his throat, into his stomach, filling him up, and pushing him out.

He's passed out before the blood vessels in his nose burst.

The following morning, the flesh that used to be Agent Wood is taken into the toilet cubicle. It lowers it's trousers and underwear, sits, and defecates. As it does so, it's eyes take in the laminated notice taped to the back of the cubicle door. It reads the words without reaction, but somewhere on the roads of America, in the refrigerated unit on the back of an eighteen wheeler, atop a mound of rotting yet still living flesh, J Edgar Hoover receives the signal from no-longer-Tom's eyes, and his face twists into a wry smile.

Please Do Not <u>Flick Blood</u> On The Walls.

Chum
Nathan Robinson

He awoke to find that both of his legs were missing.

Stumps, that was the word he was looking for. Everything below his knees was gone. The fresh wounds had been dressed, though the bandages were damp with blood. He could smell barbeque, salt and petrol all intermingling to form a unique masculine perfume.

Danny Crumb shrieked as he took in his surroundings, the strange realisation sinking in that he was on a boat, and that the boat was at sea, the early evening horizon tilting to and fro in the distance.

He was alone in this nightmare. He looked around at the small deck of the boat, and at the various paraphernalia that came with a small, sea going craft. Buckets, coils of rope, battered toolboxes.

It was the *Crispy Duck*, Hayden's boat, his girlfriend's father's boat to be precise. *But why in the hell was he on it?*

He tried to move, but found his progress halted by the fact both of his wrists were cable tied to the railing of the boat. Crumb pulled on his hands, getting nothing but resistance and tightening pain for his efforts. A surging desperation surged up from within, causing him to whimper and give a loose howl as he tugged harder and harder on his bound hands.

He was stuck fast. Not only that, he was stark bollock naked as the day he was born.

Christ, he felt drunk.

He wondered if he was so mashed that he'd imagined his legs away. He could still feel a tingle in his toes. His legs were still there, he just couldn't see them. Maybe a hole had been cut in the deck of the boat and his lower legs resided beneath him, the bandages merely a border to the illusion.

He leant back on his rump and lifted his stumps. His legs ended at the bloody bandages. It wasn't a trick of the eye, but still, he had to check.

As he drew breath to scream, a figure stepped out from the pilot house beside him, standing in front of the setting sun.

"Hello Danny," the figure spoke with a voice that was both chilling and familiar, authoritative, but calm.

Hayden Cross stepped forward and out from the glare that was burning behind him. Danny squinted to dull the light and saw a darkness upon his future father-in-law's shirt. It was awash with blood that somehow Danny knew to be his own. A lit cigar glowed and fumed from the corner of his mouth and he held a tumbler of what looked like whiskey in one hand, the ice cubes delicately chiming with the motion of the boat. He grinned; big teeth, bright and sardonic.

"How's your sea legs, Danny?" Hayden's lips bunched up as he struggled to hold in a grin, then started to guffaw at his own joke.

"Was this you?" Danny whined. "Did you fucking do this?" He tugged on the cable ties futilely.

"Who else?" the old man puffed thick smoke that was carried away by the wind. His gaze bore down on Danny. He remained silent, awaiting a response. In the meantime, he removed the cigar and tapped the ash over the side of the boat.

"Why?" Danny asked after a moment.

"Why the fuck not," Hayden shrugged.

"But why?"

"Because I don't like you Danny," Hayden said calmly. "You're not good enough for my daughter. Every time I look at you, I feel a little bit ill. You make me want to vomit."

"I think that's for her to decide, you sick fucking bastard! Now take me back to shore and give me my fucking legs back!"

Tears had started to stream down Danny Crumb's plump, red cheeks. His bottom lip trembled like that of a scorned child, which mentally, he was.

"No. We're on a fishing trip, remember? We're fishing."

Danny's mind reeled as a memory came back to him from the haze. He and Lucy had been with her parents. On a drunken night at *The Ship Inn*, Hayden had suggested a fishing trip in order to cement some future father and son-in-law bonding. Of course Danny had agreed. It was a free trip and there was a chance of getting wasted. He couldn't say no. Hayden had paid for the holiday after all. Now look at them.

"I never did anything to you," Danny whimpered.

"No. Not I. My daughter. Your behaviour is abhorrent."

"What does a bore rent mean?"

Hayden rolled his eyes. "It means that you're not a nice guy. It means that the way you carry yourself is detestable to others. I don't like the way you treat my daughter.

You've cheated on her numerous times. You borrow money without paying it back. You suggested a joint account after three dates, for fucks sake. Quite frankly you're a bum and Lucy deserves much better. To put it plain and simple, I don't like you Danny."

Danny tried to hold back the waterworks, but as his father-in-law revealed his true feelings, the well overflowed and tears spilt in rivulets down his cheeks.

"You're going to prison for this, you horrible old cunt. You're getting locked up. You're going to fucking rot there when they find out what you've done."

"Sticks and stones, Danny. Sticks and stones may break my bones, but a hacksaw can cut your fucking legs off." Hayden laughed again, dropping his hands to his knees as he struggled to contain his mirth. The laughter wetted and mutated into a cough. He started to hack, and moved to the edge of the boat and spat a dark wad overboard, coughed more, then carried on laughing before replacing the cigar to his mouth, fuming fresh, acrid smoke, a hand held to his side as if he had a stitch.

"Danny. The cops won't ever catch me. I can assure you of that." Hayden glared with his grey watery eyes as they steeled to seriousness. Danny blubbered as he struggled to accept what was going on.

"You want a drink? I've got a twenty-eight-year-old scotch."

"I don't like whiskey."

"I'm offering you some fine booze. I highly suggest that you take me up on the offer."

"Stick it up your shit pipe, you fucking psycho. You should quit drinking before your liver gives in," Danny seethed. He bared his teeth, grimacing like a mean dog. It was the best he could do.

Hayden shrugged and drained what was left in the glass.

"Quit drinking? You're probably right, scotch isn't the answer, but neither is having a salad."

He replaced the cigar in between his teeth and headed back into the pilothouse. He returned a moment later with a refilled glass, complete with fresh ice. He stepped next to Danny, knelt down then reached forward, his hand moving towards his ear as if about to pull a magic coin from behind it. Instead he jabbed something sharp into the soft flesh of his neck.

Danny yelped and recoiled, pulling away from the hot touch of the needle.

"I'm going to need another drink before the next bit." Hayden said, standing up.

Danny looked up at his captor as an unnatural warmth radiated from his neck.

"What is this shit?"

"A mild sedative. It'll knock you out for an hour. It won't take me long."

"For what?"

"You'll see."

"What have you done?" Danny asked as the sky began to tilt.

"Fuck em, Danno."

Danny had more questions, but found his thoughts slurring and sticking to one another. Above, the sky darkened, but the sun hadn't quite set yet.

He felt a tug. It was dark, he could feel nothing but a numb tug on his arm as if someone was trying to pull him up.

Then a noise.

A grating noise that rasped through his bones the way a dentist's drill is felt throughout the body in that demanding shrill. He wanted to shiver, but felt himself lost in the darkness, the grating roaring in his ears the only thing he could sense.

Danny fought to open his eyes. Pushing them up was a Herculean task and his mind screamed in frustration at his lack of sight.

He felt pain. Faraway. A warmth in his neck that spread to his arms, becoming a tightness that was slowly crushing him. His hands felt cold and he had a sense of his life leaving him, drawing away from him.

Then.

Peace. But life still leaving in drops.

A calm overtook him, but it didn't feel real; as if his body was lying to him.

Then a new sensation, one that seemed to be inside him, inside his arm. A heat. The hottest heat that soon simmered to a warmth. He thought of barbeque.

The smell of cooked food roused him from his forced slumber and he opened his eyes.

Something was pressed onto the end of what was left of his arm. Steam was rising from the flat metal base, smells of hot cooking meat were blown into his nostrils, churning his stomach with traitorous gestations.

It was his arm.

A hot iron was pressed hard onto the end of his now severed left arm and was in the process of steam sealing a fresh wound. Cable ties had been tied tight before the wound in an attempt to staunch the escaping blood which sizzled and spat hotness at his face.

The noise.

The noise was cooking bacon, sizzling and oh so tempting.

Danny looked up and saw Hayden's face caught in a grimace of concentration. His stare didn't flinch from the wound to the patient. He was locked in with his task.

His gorge rose like a rollercoaster, clogging his scream in his throat. His eyes rolled back, then he tumbled back into a now familiar darkness.

He awoke tired. The taste of old vomit plagued his tongue. Every atom of his being ached and sang with pain as if he'd had an hour on a fast spin. Drawing breath, he felt a constriction around his chest, pressing down and restricting his movements.

Danny Crumb opened his eyes to near dark. The skies above bruised purple that deepened before his eyes. He felt cold and naked, because he was cold and naked. Numbness prevailed in his fingers, but he could move his arms. He no longer felt the binds that held him to the rail. He was free.

Reaching out to grip the deck, he found his hand moving through the wood as he were a ghost, as if matter didn't matter. Danny turned to look at his left arm to discover why he felt such numbness. He expected to see the cable ties cutting off the circulation to his wrists.

He was wrong.

Fresh cable ties had been cinched tight above his elbow, below which the rest of the limb was missing.

The skin of his elbow was dark with blood, the outer flesh forming a black ridge of crust. Looking to his right, he found another absence of half-limb. He looked left, double-taking back to the right again, expecting the phantom limbs to reappear after divorcing from the rest of him.

He blinked. Gulped like a fish. Tears pooled and broke free as blood rushed to his head and changed the pressure inside his skull, forcing the water out.

"Looking for something?" Hayden asked. Danny's head jerked towards his father-in-law, who was sitting on the back of the boat, illuminated by lantern, hands bloody all the way up to the elbows, a half bottle of whiskey on the deck by his feet.

"Your arms and legs are in this bucket," Hayden stated, pointing to a plastic yellow container at his feet. Danny didn't immediately recognise the bloody stumps sticking up and out from the bucket, though he saw no reason for disbelief. The facts were that his future father-in-law had drugged him, taken his out to sea and cut his arms and legs off below the joint.

"You're fucking crazy!" Danny attempted to scream, but only managed a hoarse cry as more tears swelled and broke from his eyes.

"So you keep saying, but it's not getting you your arms and legs back. I'm so far from crazy, I've never been saner." Hayden smiled, then bent down behind the bucket and brought up a deflated, orange armband. He put the valve to his lips and started to blow. Danny lay whimpering and watched like a fat white seal, as Hayden inflated the armband, then three more.

"What are you going to do with me?" Danny eventually asked with a sense of finality.

"It's what I'm currently doing to you. We've already started. We are in the midst of it."

"But…"

"Do you know what I did for a living?"

"You're an animal doctor, I think."

"Yes, that's right Danny, I'm an animal doctor. Or as the rest of mankind refers to the profession, a vet."

"Oh yeah."

"I would've given you stitches. I've done it a million times with spayed cats, and dogs that had ripped their guts open on barb wire after running from their owners. As long as I've got the material, I can stitch anything together. But using an old iron on high is a much faster way to seal a wound when you're not that concerned about infection setting in."

"I don't deserve this."

"Lucy doesn't deserve you. She deserves much, much better. I'm making sure of that before I go."

"You can't kill me!" Danny cried. "It's fucking murder! You'll never see your daughter again."

"I've already said goodbye."

With that, Hayden leant down into the bucket of limbs and fished out a foot, then pushed it through one of the armbands with a comical squeak as it caught on the dry blood, and tossed it overboard.

"Danny, I have cancer. I'm dying. And so are you." Hayden held his gaze on Danny. It didn't falter. He was deadpan. Stone faced and as serious a heart attack.

Danny started to weep again, as if having his arms and legs cut off wasn't enough to hammer home the realisation that his fate was to end in these waters.

"I know about the money you borrowed from Lucy to fund your gambling habits."

"I can pay it back!" he pleaded.

"I know about the drink and drugs. I know that you made her get an abortion. My grandchild. You made her kill my grandchild. Thanks Danny. You dick."

"We weren't ready."

"I know that you raped her pretty much the week after she got rid of it."

"I never raped her!"

"No, she never called it rape. She couldn't bring herself to say it. She said you were piss-eyed drunk and you didn't give her a choice to say no. That's rape in my book, buddy."

"I was grieving. For the baby!" Danny cried out. Free of his bonds, he had the run of the boat. He flopped over onto his front, attempting to crawl away from his aggressor, much like a pitiful seal from the hunter's club.

Hayden laughed, loud and hearty into the air of the approaching night, as a flopping Danny made his escape attempt. He moved after him, grabbing the strap of his life vest and dragging him out of the wheelhouse and back towards the stern.

"Listen, I'm sorry. I didn't want it to end like this. I can't die and leave you to your own devices with Lucy." Hayden let go of the strap. Danny rolled onto his back and started swiping out pathetically with his stumps. Hayden stepped back.

"I couldn't do it to her. She deserves better. You know that Danny. Her grief for you will be lost in her grief for me. You'll be forgotten, and one day she'll move on."

Hayden picked the other foot from the bucket and fed it through another armband and tossed it over. He did the same with both of the forearms, shaking the hands in a gruesome wave at Danny before throwing them overboard.

"Didn't you want to wave goodbye?" Hayden smiled, reaching into his pocket, he removed a scalpel, then knelt down between Danny's legs, the blade aimed at his exposed crotch. He grabbed hold of the shrivelled penis, pulling it taut.

"There's something else I need to throw overboard before the main event."

"Oh god!" Danny recoiled, starting to shuffle back away from the sharpness of the blade. "Not my cock, man! Leave my fucking cock where it is."

"How about cock and balls?"

"No. Please. I'm sorry."

"Ahh, you're all dick, Danny. There's no brains in there. I'll leave your baby dick alone. You're not in any pain are you? You're comfortable?"

"Pain? You've cut my fucking legs off! You've cut my fucking arms off for christssake!"

"But does it hurt?"

Danny took a moment. He looked at his stumps quizzically.

"No pain?" Hayden asked. "Just numb? A little groggy."

"Well yeah."

"So technically I've not hurt you?"

"Well no, but you still cut my limbs off you mad, daft cunt!" Danny screeched. "I think that matters in the grand scheme of things."

"No it doesn't." Hayden took a swig from the near empty bottle. He offered the dregs to Danny.

"Want some?"

"Fuck off."

"Any last words. Not that anyone else will hear them."

"Fuck off."

"Original."

Hayden drank the rest, following it with a happy gasp. He picked up another bottle from behind the bucket and twisted the cap off with a curt snap, letting the cap drop to the deck. From the top pocket of his shirt he took out a blister pack of pills. He popped them all out and slung them into his mouth, chasing them down with a slug of scotch.

He smiled at Danny for maybe a minute or so, holding the strange grimace intently.

No words.

Until.

"So, what are you gonna do Danny?" Hayden drawled. "I've cut off your fucking legs."

"Please. If you're gonna kill me, just kill me. Quit torturing me already. Quit fucking about. This is horrible."

Hayden half smiled in a grin that didn't quite stretch across his mouth. The scotch had taken hold; the pills would be next.

"I'm not going to kill you, that was never my intention."

"Thank fuck."

Hayden tossed the scalpel overboard and walked past Danny, towards the wheelhouse. He emerged seconds later with a petrol canister and a sinister, sloppy smile.

"I suggest you put any swimming lessons to good use."

Danny watched in chilled, treacle slow horror as Hayden uncapped the fuel canister and began to pour the clear liquid on the floor of the wheelhouse.

"Maybe they'll see the smoke, maybe they won't. Either way, the boat will be gone. And so will we."

Hayden reached down and picked up another fuel canister. He popped the top with the same expression on his face as if he were opening another bottle of scotch. Giggling, he stepped towards Danny, lifting the can over his limbless body and began to pour the fuel, christening him with the potential of fire.

Danny recoiled as the liquid stung his eyes, struggling away as the fuel seeped between his stitches and flared up fresh pain at his severed nerve endings, causing him to howl and spit and choke and swear in a thousand different languages. He swung his phantom arm over the edge of the boat and lifted his weight with an agonising strain that popped the warm crust of his wound.

"Best get swimming Danny!" Hayden laughed as he deposited the last dregs of fuel on Danny's back as he struggled to his stumps.

He raised his other half-arm, locking on and pulling himself up and pressing his weight on the flaps of knee skin that were now his feet. He pushed and pulled, no matter the pain, it was worth it to escape the clutches of this madman.

With a final exhausting struggle, he got his chest over the edge, wriggling until his gut rested instead. Tipping his weight forward, the dark skin of the water rushing up to meet him, hitting his face like a slab, the shock of the cold on his injuries followed.

Swallowed by the murky abyss, Danny Crumb flopped beneath the surface, his invisible hands clawing for purchase that wasn't there, his feet kicking out at a surface that would never hold his husky weight.

With a bubbling scream, he choked. He punched out as the white panic overtook the yawning darkness. He felt his entire skin (what he had left), including his testicles, tighten and shrink in response to the cold as they knotted up and crawled into him. Sea water invaded his lungs as he fought the urge to breathe. The debate raging of whether or not to take a breath, though he knew, no matter what, he shouldn't. A single inhale would kill him.

As he pondered this fateful decision, he felt the pressure change as his face broke the surface. Instinct fought necessity and he coughed and heaved a breath simultaneously, dragging the falling water into his mouth.

The life vest. That's what had brought him to the surface. Danny took another breath, slowing the kicks of his impotent legs. He relaxed some, letting the vest take his weight as he shifted trust.

A rushing WHUMP sound brushed his ears. He turned back to the boat. A bright ball of flame raging upwards into the night; The *Crispy Duck* was alight. The engine still chugged as it moved away from him. A splash caused him to turn to the left, where he met a maniacal face moving towards him. It was Hayden, swimming one-handed, a bottle of scotch in his other hand, raised above the water line to avoid contamination. He took a swig then spat it out with a laugh into Danny's face.

"Have a drink!" Hayden laughed madly, eyes goggling with a crazed glint in the moonlight and fleeing fire.

"Get the fuck away from me!" Danny lunged forward as Hayden grabbed hold of his vest, anchoring himself. Misjudging the attack, Danny's face connected with the old man's forehead, his nose popped like an overripe tomato. Danny wailed and Hayden laughed, his forehead speckled with fresh blood which washed off in the next splash of seawater.

"Do you know why we're here Danny?"

"Because you're a fucking psycho!"

"No. Not the situation. The location?"

"Get off me, you nutcase. I don't fucking care."

"Global warming has made the oceans warmer, not just rise. This means the water becomes more clement for other species that in the past you wouldn't usually find here."

"So fucking what. I don't give two fucks about your fish. Get off me and drown."

Hayden ignored the comment and continued. "A few hundred feet beneath us are thermal vents which attract many species not usually native to our colder waters. One of these species is the Great White Shark."

He ceased struggling and breathing as his mind processed those words. He felt his blood cool a thousand degrees and his bladder expand tenfold. He looked towards the *Crispy Duck*, then back to Hayden.

"Wh-whu-what?"

"Sharks. Great Whites. Fucking big ones!"

"You're crazy."

"No. I'm completely in control of my faculties, Danny. I'm well aware of where I am and what I'm doing. I've been planning this for months. I knew I had to stop you. Then I found out about the cancer. I was in the waiting room and read an article in *National Geographic* about the sharks off the south coast of England. It's strange how fate works."

Hayden grasped hold of Danny's life jacket and pulled him close.

"The pieces fit. How could I not?"

"You're insane." The more Danny repeated that statement, the less he believed it himself. Hayden wasn't taking notice of his opinion.

"I've told you, I'm not."

Danny looked over Hayden's shoulder at the rapidly vanishing boat. It was a distant flame heading out into the Atlantic.

I could make it, Danny thought. *I could paddle to the boat and climb on. I could put the fire out. I'd be safe. Somehow.*

Danny pushed Hayden away with his charred stumps. He hit the old man so hard the wound split further and a jolt of numbed agony shot up his half arm. He squealed, but didn't let it stop his escape. Hayden lunged for Danny, but with being woozy from the booze and pills he missed and headed beneath the water.

"Danny! Come back! I'm not finished."

They both swam towards the flaming boat for different reasons and with very different swimming styles. A splash to Danny's left instilled him with a plague of fresh fear.

"Danny boy! Let's talk like men. We need to sort this out!"

Hayden hadn't left the boat in full speed, but it idled away at a walking pace. If he kept up this armless paddle, he might make it.

The boat was turning in a wide circle. All he had to do was swim to where it was heading and close the distance.

He was bleeding from every stump, splashing dementedly towards his goal.

"Danny!" Hayden called. "Come back fella!"

An explosion of water erupted behind Danny. There was a yelp then a second splash as something heavy and long hit the water.

He turned to face the darkening waters. The last burnt ochre from the distant sun cast a wide sparkle of spaced glitters amongst the rising and falling foam.

Hayden was gone.

Shapes bobbed atop waves. A hand waved in silhouette.

It took him a moment to realise he was waving at himself.

Danny laughed, then Danny cried exhaustive tears.

He almost waved back to complete the circle of weirdness, but then he remembered he didn't have any hands in which to reciprocate the strange greeting.

He blubbered before resuming his pursuit of the fleeing boat. He wanted to give up. To just cry and for everything to turn black and be over. But hope and fear herded him on until exhaustion would take him down.

The flames had fully engulfed the wheelhouse of the *Crispy Duck* and Danny could but watch as the boat slowed, an explosion bloomed up, striving to touch the night sky.

He ambled and watched as over the space of a minute, the vessel listed, then sank rapidly, the water extinguishing the inferno with a bitter hiss, taking any light down with it.

He stopped his swim to take stock, leaning back and letting the life jacket take his weight in the water.

It didn't.

Danny gasped as he felt himself fall beneath the surface, the depths pulling him under.

The jacket didn't fit anymore. It was snug when he'd threw himself into the water, but now it apparently didn't. The strap had loosened; or perhaps Hayden had unclipped it when he'd grabbed hold of him. *The cunt.* Either way, the vest was loose and he hadn't the dexterity to clip it back on with his neat little, bloody stumps.

He fought for the surface, waving his propulsion-free, untrained limbs through the cold darkness. He felt the pressure change, emerging into the different darkness of the cloudy night sky.

Danny shrieked wordlessly up at the far, billowing clouds because he couldn't think of anything else to do.

Hope. That was all he had left.

And that was fading in flurries of fear.

Light had left when the boat sank and the sun had set for the evening.

His already depleted energy was fading.

But hope. He had an endless abundance of that.

A boat might come, a helicopter might see the wreckage, or he might wake from this nightmare.

Not once did he think anything positive about Lucy, the girlfriend he'd cheated on, stolen from, abused and generally been a complete shit to.

Even in this dark moment, before an inevitable death, he didn't consider Lucy the best thing that had happened to him. He thought in a blind rage that this was somehow her fault, even though she remained apparently oblivious to her father's scheme.

The cunt.

That fucking cunt.
That stupid fat fucking cunt.
She'd put him up to this.

It was her. She hated him. The last time he'd hit her, a nice hard and flat smack across the cheeks, he'd seen the hate burning back at him. He'd had a sense of retaliation from her that she might suddenly stop and hold him accountable for what she'd made him do to her.

It was her.
It must be.

As Danny pointlessly considered how he'd gotten himself into this predicament, a freight train hit him from below. Pushed up with such force, he erupted from the water a good three metres; so high in fact, he managed a glimpse of the spinning sunset as it peaked its last for the day beyond the horizon.

A dark shape moved up with him, rolling to reveal a ghost white belly. The derailing train that had hit him was shark-shaped. He span again, then slapped hard back onto the water, a searing coolness invading his insides, the warmth leaving him. This was more than just pain.

Something body-warm slithered up and along his chest and up to his neck.

Sausage skin, he thought as the only way to describe the slick feel, then it dawned on him that he was unspooling, his guts falling freely and unravelling from his inside and into the dark press of the ether.

All light vanished.

The life vest was gone, and now he was falling, sinking into nothingness.

He screamed frantic bubbles, into the black veil as he drowned for the last time.

Things became darker as he choked on brine and gut blood, his brain becoming starved of oxygen.

But not before the ancient predator hit him again, teeth shredding through his already broken body, bones splintering like balsa.

He felt every bite until the last.

The shark had struck Hayden on the back of his legs, the teeth grazing and shearing the meat off his calf.

He spent a moment underwater, returning to the surface after getting his bearings and figuring which way was up.

Danny had left him, continuing his futile escape towards the fleeing, burning, sinking boat.

But then Hayden had smiled as the Great White breached, pushing Danny free from the water with the tip of its nose, teeth gnashing. Details were lost in the twilight, but despite it being sudden, Hayden felt the power of the giant silhouette as it emerged, stunning its prey with a bouldering charge from below.

He had always wanted to see that.

The fact that it was his dickhead of a future son-in-law made it even sweeter.

The smile creased further as the dark water exploded around him, as his own predator returned, an open mouth surging up from the darkness.

He didn't scream as the teeth gnashed and cut and tore through his tumor riddled body.

Safe in knowledge that his daughter was free of that terrible, piss poor excuse of a man, he smiled for a final time, for he was cured.

The Bearded Woman
Alessandro Manzetti

(Translated into English by Daniele Bonfanti)

Midday. Syrena, the Bearded Woman of the Suprême, heats up a grenadine of orange crystals in the large silt-static ignition pan, a cult item for circus trailers; her red bean soup, kept inside her fridge inside flexible water cans with a variable-value tag: *Expiré le 3 Février, 37 p.U.* Three years ago.

"Armand? Armand!" The lady is restless.

"I'm here, sweetmeat," the dwarf answers in a syrupy voice, hopping and popping his miniature jaws.

"Stop doing that hideous noise, you know I can't stand it!" the woman groans; she is the size of a career gladiator. "Have you bought sweet potatoes?" she immediately adds, scratching her right breast.

"But…honey, you know this morning I had rehearsals for the donkey show, how could I…"

"*Fuck, fuck and fuck!* I should have married Mister Skeleton, not a flea like you… He still fondles my ass, you know? That's a real man…"

"Sure, sure…twenty years ago, *maybe*," the proud dwarf defends himself. "Since they installed the Fabergè electric pick in his prostate, he can hardly walk, all spread-legged…and he pisses more than a horse. It's those discharges, you know, that contraption doesn't work well… That's what you get when you do surgery in a garage…"

"You're only jealous – always have been. That's a real man, let me tell you. And next time he fondles, I'm spreading my thighs for him… Knowing that, maybe you'll get hard again too, *Mister Flea*."

"But, sweetmeat, what are you saying?" the tiny man whines. "All this fuss over three kilos of sweet potatoes, *eh*?"

"I'm serious. *No potatoes? Spread thighs. Understood?* Let me think about his prostate… I'm going to work that stud with gusto. Just let me finish cooking this shit and feed the kids… that noble ancestry of donkey tamers you had me dump on the Earth. You'll have to live with it, and don't you come watch…"

Armand's cheeks turn red, unlike the violet tomatoes in the bowl close to the woman, dark and weirdly chromed like every vegetable on their table, coming from the illegal magnetic-induction greenhouses in district 4. Though their circus wages aren't half bad, they certainly cannot afford New Scotland products. Clean products. The little man squeezes his diminutive fists, pops his jaws again and assaults the calves of his granitic wife. A bite, then two more. Not even a piranha would be that quick and lethal.

"Son of a bitch!" she screams, bucking, while her precious red beard dips a few centimeters into the by-now boiling soup. "Jesus, look what you've done. If this gets burned, I'm losing my job…shitty flea. *Let me catch you!*"

A Satanic sneer on her face – like a billy-goat to whom they have just snatched a testicle – she grabs a knife and chases her husband, making the trailer rock. Two dogs out there, guarding the empty air set beneath the yellowish sky, begin barking, almost resurrecting.

"*Stop, or this time I'll charge double!*"

The tiny man zigzags around the table, like a rabbit with its ass on fire; he must find his *wife tamer* before she grasps his neck, or he will be in trouble. He hid it under the cube of the kids' entertainment system. The she-bison is strong, but slow; he kneels on the carpet, reaches out and finds the Holy Grail of the sons of a lesser and drunken god, the instrument turning any South Paris 5 dwarf into a superman. He stops shaking and stands, brandishing – with glittering eyes – his electric cat-o'-nine-tails.

"*Come here, sweetmeat...*" he hisses, like a cobra ready to strike.

Red button? No, come on: killing her would be too much, the usual lesson will be enough...blue button it is. The cat-o'-nine-tails sucks energy in a single breath, excitedly vibrating; LEDs light up on the tips of the claw-shaped whips, then its induction lead spheres animate themselves. Flagellation, without going too far, and then a nice screw to make peace; Armand's usual schedule, whenever he forgets buying something for his neurasthenic corsair bride. *Jesus Christ, sweet potatoes!*

The Bearded Woman pulls up short, staring at that hellish device as it flares up in the hand of the man of the house. "*Bastard...*" she whispers, already exhausted, blood squirting backward in her veins, filling up too soon her disproportionate head; just at the sight of the flail, she feels her back and buttocks burn like hell.

"You know how this is going to go down, right, *sweetmeat?*"

The little man swings his portable Armageddon upward, popping his jaws to infuriate his wife even more, as she stays unmoving like a presidential guard, the tips of her pink slippers on the imaginary red line of pain, on the threshold. *She is going to pass it, it is going to hurt.* Outside, the ghost dogs keep barking; the smaller, contaminated by strange purple stains on his back – you really shouldn't suck on bones buried in Uxor-sick dirt – leaps forward and approaches the flexible water window of trailer 7. He wants to enjoy the scene, his paws laying on the laminal gap where sludge flows, and his tail up straight.

The dwarf stops lingering; he articulates his shoulder and bends in baseball-pitcher pose, ready to unleash the flail on the woman's massive body, as she foams rage-bubbles from the corners of her mouth. But something does not work: an invisible motherfucker – the same wraith which scared the dogs outside? – snatches the cat-o'-nine-tails off his hand, sucking it upward. Armand raises his eyes on the low ceiling of his mobile home, and sees the clawed rosary – his only weapon – coiled up among the blades of the fan. It's been goddamn hot, these last few days, and the fixing up of the environmental temperature generator has ended up somewhere with Syrena's sweet potatoes. The blame falls on the donkeys, with their phosphorescent reins and their semi-organic saddles with silvery fringes, affixed to their back via hinges grafted to their spines – may Michelet be blessed for his invention of the neural screw, better than prehistoric Jenner and his smallpox vaccine – and antimony sulfate around their big, stupid bluish eyes. Beasts demanding daily care and training.

Unarmed, the dwarf grins to the Bearded Woman, showing her the small piano wedged in his mouth, made of yellow and black teeth, while its hammers beat on his palate making him stammer, his quick little eyes pointed on her knife – he tries to say something useful: "Can we skip directly to making peace, this time?"

Clenching her teeth, his wife advances walking wide-legged, slowly rocking, as though she wore jeans with a too-narrow crotch – maybe she is possessed by John Wayne's holo-ghost. She grabs the donkey tamer by his hair, lifts him up and takes him close to her big rage-flaming face, perfectly matching her polished violet lipstick and reddish beard.

"It's you who doesn't know how this is going to go down, *big man…*" she says to him in a hoarse voice, then turning back to check the sizzling pan. The soup is burning, goodbye. "You're worse than plague…see what you've done? Not only will I spread my thighs for Mister Skeleton, but your nice white belly too…"

While Armand tries to struggle out of the she-bison's grasp, jerking like a jack-in-the-box with his feet in the air, she sinks her knife in his still-empty stomach, spits in his face and drops him, deflated, on the floor.

The man twists on the ground, his short-fingered hand trying to plug the gash; he is dying accompanied by a strange soundtrack: the overheating fan engine, bogged down in the wife-tamer's tails. It rustles and buzzes like a hornet about to explode in a little glass trap – the last sounds he will hear, besides the *blops* of the bitch's knife that keeps raging upon him, everywhere, with its ham blade. The dwarf was hoping, whenever the moment came for him to cross the blue gate, to be accompanied by the bray of his donkey friends: Ingres, Monet, and Cézanne; those beasts have always respected him, more than any bipedal of his life, kids included; tailed angels with brains cooked by radiation and contaminated horse feed. How good they were, as they marched during the show.

Blop, again, and then *sguash*, his throat. The blue gate appears, just like Armand had pictured it, but he cannot even reach up to the doorknob to get on the other side.

Will they have a circus in Limbo? And donkeys, maybe?

*Everything burnt: no lunch, and the kids are about to be back, I'll have to make do…*Syrena thinks, rubbing her beard, soiled with the unlucky guy's guts. She cleans her hands on the kitchen apron, adorned with drawn plums, and she watches her husband's disarranged body, there on the floor, his eyes still hooked to that cursed fan. *And now I also have to clean all this mess…who knew a fucking dwarf could have so much blood…there's liters! I could as well have slaughtered a hippo!*

Seconds pass, the woman looks out of the trailer window and sees the two dogs, trained to survival, quickly scuttle toward the Baden landfill, until they vanish behind the first towers which lean on their foundations of rags, junk, and old spare parts. Down there, a little on the left, she seems to see a grey-silver rainbow arching between the molecular burners – the great nibblers of the past. It looks like a scythe blade, actually, or a giant meat cleaver ready to drop down on what used to be, what still moves, breathes, in that graveyard, under its flying horizon shaken by the flapping wings of the cloacal gulls.

Cowards! So be it, she mutters in her thoughts, *we need a special menu…piglet roast. Of dwarf. After all, we have to celebrate. I'm going to have a real man around, now, and a lot of bags of sweet potatoes. But now let's think about the kids.*

"*Mmm…* smells good!"

"What's that?"

"*Mom, mom, Monet slapped me!*"

"Be quiet, and don't touch anything; wash your hands, change your shirt and then sit down at the table. You little piglets!" Syrena groans, brandishing a wooden spoon toward the empty heads of the three kids. Ingres, Cézanne, and Monet – the abusive one. That's right, Armand named them like his dancing donkeys. "Come on, hurry up. *Special menu today…*"

The woman has set everything properly, even though it is not Sunday. The good dish set, enameled cutlery – Mister Skeleton's wedding gift – and Armand as center-piece: arms and legs cut off and an apple between his teeth, nicely roasted. You can no longer recognize him, after the treatment; his wife has worked hard with the

Metzelder carver, then she has seasoned the poor devil with pink rosemary, mustard icing and an abundant dose of her signature spicy sauce, purple like a priest's mourning. It only lacks a pretty circle of chopped sweet potatoes, all around, then the picture would be perfect. *Dwarf stew à la Corse.* The tiny man still seems to be looking upward, toward the fan blades, with his little blue eyes goggling and sucked out by the suction cups of the oven's 750 degrees. He lays on the silver platter, the one with Syrena's mother's initials on the edge: L.B., one of the early stars of the Suprême: *Lady Blackbeard.* Too bad she croaked untimely, trying to strangulate her husband with his own guts after ripping open his belly with her teeth – she had caught him in bed with an Egyptian contortionist, a pearl necklace around his stout neck and a radioactive kiwi up his ass. Heart attack, right in the thick of it. A real badass bearded woman.

"Good! I want more!" Ingres, the youngest, brays.

"Don't choke on it, eat slowly," his mother commands, cleaning the orange gravy off her beard; thick like mortar.

"*Fuck*, you have to buy more of this shit!" Chubby Cézanne jumps on his seat, struck down by wet taste-bud rapture, before getting another slap on his neck by his rough brother.

The she-bison groans, "*Hey, is that a way to talk?* If your father was here, you'd see...and if you don't quit fighting, you two, *I'll put you in the oven.*" Then, she stops a moment to think about that, her fork two centimeters away from her mouth and a piece of her husband's ear down in her belly, melting away like *foie gras*, releasing an acid broth of deep mocking. But.

Goddamn, and who knew dwarves were so tasty? You'd never believe that! she thinks, then beginning to eagerly watch, with predator eyes, her own offspring; Armand's kids. *Same breed, same meat. But they must be even tastier, when they're little. Who cares, I did them and now I can gobble them up...they're* my *stuff.*

102

Syrena crosses herself, gets up waving her red-orange beard over the tits which have worked so much and have now surrendered to gravity, letting themselves be sucked in toward the floor like giant dried plums. *Milk, day and night,* she remembers, *suck, suck and suck...they never had enough. Dwarves as hungry as wolves, how the fuck can they eat so much and stay so little? I used to have breasts straight and taut like a boat prow, and Mister Skeleton drooled over them. Time for a makeover* – thanks to poor Armand's savings: she well knows where he took his stash – *hard as marble...and a crackerjack dinner.*

"So, kids, let's do a funny game. Dad is coming home soon: let's hide in the kitchen, so we pop out when he enters to scare him, okay? Come on, piglets, come with Mom…"

As Cézanne grabs his mother's hand to join her in the game, the Bearded Woman cannot resist and pinches the boy's fat ass, a nice protein pudding, and she eagerly licks her lips.

"Come on, sweetheart. Let's hurry."

Finger Paint
Robert Essig

Bradley Jenkins took a balled fist to the face like using his nose to catch a bag of sand. It hurt, but was certainly not the first punch he'd taken in a life that was more uphill both ways than anything.

Josh Decker taunted him. "Bradley faggly, take your lumps, bitch!"

Josh thought he was clever, but Bradley had heard that one since his schoolmates learned the effectiveness of negative slurs. This ragged crew of vagabonds that always hovered around Josh like flies at a dump laughed as if on cue. Probably didn't even find the comment funny, just knew the right place to insert the laughter that made their brute leader happy. Truth was they were scared of Josh. Didn't want to find themselves on the receiving end of his well-seasoned knuckles.

After years of abuse at the hands of Josh and other such bullies, Bradley had learned to take his lumps like a man. Instinct told him to drop to the ground and roll into a ball to protect his face, gut, and the family jewels, but often times that instigated a group beating. The hangers-on liked to kick a guy while he was down.

Another knuckle-duster. Bradley saw stars.

"Yuck," said Josh. "Don't want to get his blood on me. Pussy blood belongs on a tampon!"

Josh gave Bradley a shove, and though he'd been holding his own against the onslaught of fists, he fell to the ground in a sniveling heap of damaged youth. As Josh glowered, rubbing his knuckles, his pals—Joey, Mitch, and Danny—kicked Bradley in the ribs. Their attack was half hearted and soon enough the four bruisers were gone, leaving Bradley crying and curled in a fetal position.

The cheery chirping of birds that had been disrupted during the assault returned, but Bradley could hardly hear over his own weeping.

A hand gently touched his shoulder like a large leaf fallen from the trees above. Bradley flinched and retreated in defense. Local hobo Jenks stood there, years of age worn over his face in deep grooves, puffy bags beneath his eyes like fleshy sacks of jelly. Jenks looked surprised or even shocked, but Bradley took no consolation in the face of what could prove to be another predator.

Bradley ran.

The park was on his way home from school. His family had fallen on hard times (seemed to *live* in hard times) so he had to walk rather than take the bus. Not that the bus would have deterred the bullies from picking on him.

He ran away from his problems the way he always had. When it came to fight or flight, Bradley flew like an eagle, or perhaps more like a crippled pigeon.

He didn't want to go home. It was maybe the safest place he could think of if it wasn't for his mother and father, who would undoubtedly be fighting. That was all they did anymore. Fought about bills, finances, the neighbors, just about anything, and Bradley could hardly stand it.

At the far end of the park was a little-used bathroom facility. There was only one toilet, which meant that there was a lock. Bradley had gone to that very restroom many times before to lock himself in for safety and to clean up before going home. Going home all bloodied was bad news. His father would call him a pussy. The man never laid a hand on Bradley, but his verbal abuse knew no bounds. Bradley figured taking a few lumps would have been preferable.

The fifteen-year-old teenager that looked at Bradley through the mirror was a disgrace. A shit stain. Blood ran from his nose and lips that were fattening up. There was no way he would be able to clean himself up enough not to show what had happened to him. His father would be displeased, ashamed of a son who was more of a dreamer, an artist than a tough guy or an athlete.

Blood on his shirt. Still running out of his nose like it was thinning rather than clotting.

He blinked several times, leaning over the sink, closer to the cloudy mirror with its corners obscured by adolescent graffiti. He'd had many a bloody nose by every bully in every school he'd ever gone to, but never had the blood ran so profusely. It had been soaking into his shirt and now dripped onto the grimy sink like red drops from a defunct faucet.

Later Bradley would sit in his room recovering from his father's mental mayhem, unable to understand why he did what he'd done, what possessed him place his hands on his mouth, his nose. The first application of blood-paint was a sloppy affair. It just sort of happened. A smear here; a slathering there. Across the mirror streaks of red were strewn about, shifting until eventually they became recognizable. A face.

Bradley stood back, breathing hard as if he'd endured a great deal of strain. It took him a moment to realize whom the face belonged to, and when he did, he became filled with rage. Blood dripped from his swollen nose like rainwater from a clogged downspout.

Bradley punched the caricature he'd painted in blood. A solitary crack halved the face like a bolt of lightning. He dropped to the floor and cried, clutching his aching fist.

It wasn't the pain in his knuckles that caused the tears, but a stronger, deeper pain in his heart that he would take to bed with him that night, crying tears afresh.

Lakeside High was an uninspired series of buildings that reeked of sixties architecture and sub par education. An open campus due to the mild climate of Southern California, there were no lockers, and the kids tended to segregate themselves in groups based on everything from skin color to preference in drugs to interest in comic books to whatever else a school full of teenagers could think of to alienate themselves from one another.

Bradley was a loner, a one-man clique who often sat beneath a tree near the quad where the ASB brats mulled over who was fucking who and whatnot. Bradley always had his nose in a book, one eye on the words, the other on the lookout for potential trouble. He learned a long time ago that trouble was just a clenched fist and a hyena laugh away.

A few paragraphs into chapter five of the latest Star Trek novel, something caught his eye. He was drawn out of the book as if he hadn't been reading it at all. The bloodied mirror from yesterday flashed in his mind when he heard the boisterous rumblings of Josh and his pals. When Josh turned enough for Bradley to see his face, Bradley dropped his book, mouth agape.

Though he couldn't hear them, he could tell by their body language what Josh was talking about. It looked like a scar, but that was impossible. It must have been a lengthy scratch from an angry cat or perhaps a cut from a jagged piece of glass. Whatever it was, Bradley couldn't help but take notice of the diagonal rendering of the mysterious affliction that cut across Josh's face.

After school Bradley crossed through the park quicker than he had yesterday, looking over his shoulder for Josh, Joey, Mitch or Danny. Any one of them was bad news, but all of them together was a disaster.

Sure that they weren't following, he slipped into the bathroom at the rear of the park. He locked the door and stared into the mirror, breathless.

The blood had dried almost black. It looked more like paint today than blood. The face in the mirror was Josh's, and the crack...

The crack had Bradley thinking so hard that it took him a moment to hear the dripping.

Drip. Drip.

Today it didn't take a clenched fist to start his nose bleeding, dripping over his lips and cascading down his chin, spattering on the floor.

Using his palm, he removed as much of yesterday's painting as he could, the dried blood flaking off and floating to the sink like black dandruff.

With his canvas cleared, Bradley used both hands, slathered with blood from the inkwell that was his nose. He worked his fingers on the glass in a madcap state the masterful artists of yesteryear indulged in after years of breathing in the intoxicating fumes of oil-based lead paints. His brow perspired as fever raged, but his fingers swirled and stroked the mirror, periodically gracing his bloodied face in a manner that was akin to an out of body experience. Bradley watched his hands work as the crimson blur that overshadowed his reflection become an image, and soon enough he was finished.

He washed his hands and face and left for home.

Bradley thought a lot that night about what had happened in the park restroom. He couldn't explain the experience were someone to have found out and questioned him about what he'd painted on that mirror. He could hardly remember what the final image was. From the point his nose began to bleed, his mind entered a fugue state that he embraced with open arms, allowing himself to slip into a blood-smeared oblivion. There was comfort in that state.

The next day at school was an awkward affair. Bradley walked the halls with more melancholy than usual, averting his eyes from even attempting to look at the girls he knew he had no chance with.

At lunch he found a clearing beneath the art building awning, which overlooked an area where the ASB drama queens congregated around the statue of their school mascot, a gaudy looking eagle, that centered the quad.

Unable to lose himself in his book, Bradley watched the statue. He was drawn to it for some reason. Wanted to go up and examine it closely as if it were a masterpiece akin to Michelangelo's David.

And then he saw Josh and Danny for the first time that day. They walked onto the quad, hand in hand, a scene so unusual that hordes of students were pointing, some even giggling, though they all knew damn well to giggle in the face of Josh Decker was to giggle in the face of death.

Once Josh and Danny took position in front of the eagle statue, Bradley felt his gut tighten. He'd seen this before.

In blood.

The delinquent duo, as homophobic as they come, grasped one another like lovers. Their mouths became one, heads tilting as if what they shared was a long hidden passion that they decided to make known in a drastically public way.

The crowd gasped and for a moment there was silence across what was a routinely boisterous lunch period. Murmurs flittered like so many butterflies. There were hushed laughs and then someone yelled, "Faggots!" and laughed, which became contagious. Laughter erupted, fingers pointed, slurs were spoken.

Bradley stood on a ledge to have a good look at the spectacle. He couldn't believe what he was witnessing, and yet he knew there was more. But that couldn't happen.

It just couldn't.

Danny dropped to his knees. Josh tilted his head to the sky, eyes closed, face the epitome of passion. Danny grabbed and massaged the bulge in his pants. At this, the massive audience shushed again, shocked at what was playing out before their collective eyes. Just as Danny unzipped Josh's pants, a number of teachers and administrators rushed through the crowd, probably expecting a fight. What they encountered was so ludicrous that they stopped for a moment, just as shocked as the crowd of students, before they grabbed Danny as he was about to wrap his lips on Josh's erection.

The act of breaking them apart seemed to break the trance they had been under. Josh slammed his pants shut so hastily that he zipped the tip of his penis. That was the expletive heard 'round campus, and that was what finally snapped Bradley out of his own trance, which resulted in a bout of laughter so loud he became a bit of a spectacle himself.

Danny appeared to be dazed. Probably wondering about what must have been a bad taste left in his mouth considering the tongue kiss he'd shared with Josh, who wasn't the most hygienic guy in the world. Josh, on the other hand, singled Bradley out, and the look on his face would have given Satan a double take.

"Don't you laugh, Bradley, you fuck! You'll get yours, asshole!"

Bradley stopped laughing as if there was a switch that had been tripped. He was immediately filled with terror, however Josh was being handled by several of the PE teachers, screaming and cursing as they ushered him away.

The last two periods were the longest Bradley had ever experienced. There was no telling what happened to Josh after the incident on the quad, but Bradley knew damn well that he was on Josh's shit list. Right on top in red ink, all caps and underlined.

Bradley didn't want to take the park route home in case Josh was waiting for him. There was no way Josh could know that he was responsible for what happened, but he had this lump of guilt growing in his mind like some rapid spreading cancer.

As much as Bradley wanted to avoid the park, there was a burning desire to see what he'd painted on the bathroom mirror. He knew the image (had seen it in his mind as he watched it play out near the statue on the quad), but he had to see it in the flesh, just to make sure it was there, because what had happened…well, there was no way to explain it.

The park was dead. Always dead. It served as a shortcut for many of his fellow students but most of them preferred to take the longer route, probably so they could walk with their friends who lived closer to school. Bradley never had friends. He considered his colored pencil set his best friend. He could find a quiet place and sketch away his worries, because there were always worries. Worries at school, worries at home, worries while walking through the park.

"What are you laughing at, Bradley Faggley?"

Bradley stopped, closed his eyes and took a deep breath. Josh revealed himself from behind a tree. Bradley should have expected it. No, he *did* expect it, but he couldn't resist the force that pulled him to that bathroom.

"Where do you think you're going, asshat?"

"I'm going home."

"You think you can laugh at me and get away with it?"

Bradley stared into the face of malice. What he saw in Josh's eyes was rage incarnate. Josh enjoyed beating the shit out of the weak, and he'd been known to skin a cat or two just for the hell of it, but what lurked in those eyes was equal only to something found in the eyes of a serial killer.

Or maybe, just maybe what Bradley saw was shame. How could Josh go back to school after what happened?

That was the last thought Bradley had before he was plummeted with a barrage of fists. Only two fists, but they came down in such succession it was like there were more than one Josh.

Against his rule about remaining on his feet, Bradley involuntarily dropped.

"You like that, you little faggot! Huh? You like that!"

Bradley had been beat the fuck up before. Ended up in the hospital once, but nothing he'd experienced could have prepared him for this kind of brutality. He screamed and cried and caught a fist in his open mouth that knocked out way too many teeth. He choked on a few of them, along with so much blood that he couldn't breathe. He tried to yell that Josh was killing him, but the blows never let up, and soon enough all he could do was whine incoherently and pray for death.

Praying did nothing. Josh became frantic, hitting and screaming, spittle flying out of his mouth mixing with the blood that splashed from Bradley's distorted face.

The last thing that went through Bradley's mind as he slipped into darkness was that Josh was getting his revenge on the entire school for their laughter and taunts, directing his anger at the easiest target.

Josh finally drew himself away from the bloody body. Bradley's face couldn't have been compared to ground beef—didn't look that neat. It was more like something run over by a car and pulverized. The body was decorated with blood, but remained intact, the brunt of the beating having been directed to the face.

Josh stumbled backwards, sniffling and mumbling. He stood, bearing witness to his handiwork, and he started to cry. A hand came down on his shoulder. Josh yelped. Instinct turned him around and he met an old, grisly face with a soft, bloody punch that registered in pain.

It was Jenks.

The homeless man took a defensive step back, but Josh made no further move to harm the derelict. Rather he looked at his mangled fists and sobbed. A moment later he bolted from the park.

Jenks had seen the beating. He saw everything that happened in the park. It was his home as much as it was the home of the squirrels and the chirping birds, silent now in the wake of damning violence.

It was clear that the boy on the ground was dead. Jenks may have gotten most of his meals out of a garbage can, but he knew dead when he saw it and there was no way any living thing could survive when their face had been crumpled inward like a fender after a car wreck.

There was so much blood.

The bathroom was in the close distance. Jenks wouldn't even go in there. He'd loitered around this park for enough years to know that there was something wrong with that bathroom, something that seemed to shun the park in its entirety.

But he couldn't deny the urge he felt, so strong—no, not an urge, a desire!

Bradley had been a skinny boy, so it wasn't much a feat for Jenks to cradle his body and carry him to the restroom. Even as he opened the door, Jenks felt a mix of terror and bliss. He'd only been in there once before, many years ago after being jumped by a gang of drunk college students from up north who must have been driving through town with nothing better to do. He'd taken refuge in there because the door had a lock and they couldn't get to him. They banged and taunted, yelled and even climbed on top. He'd thought for sure that they were going to break the door down, but eventually they tired of the charade and left. Jenks had been so terrified that he'd curled himself into a ball on the floor and went to sleep. He'd dreamt that his tormentors were slaughtered violently, but it was more of a nightmare, and when he woke he was in complete darkness, disoriented and frightened. He'd screamed and cried until he finally gained his bearings, unlocked the door, and left the bathroom never to return.

Until now.

Inside, it smelled faintly like copper. Jenks was taken aback by the crude yet legible artwork on the walls and mirror: Two young men standing before a giant eagle. In one drawing they were kissing. In another drawing one guy was on his knees giving the other a hummer.

But Jenks hardly had more than a fleeting glimpse of the images before he found himself inside the bathroom with the bloodied body. He locked the door. The day's heat had dried the blood on the walls and mirror to the point of cracking and flaking off. Jenks used his hands to swipe away the dried blood. He then used the boy's crushed face like a palette (though it was more like a crude bowl), dipping his fingers in the pooled blood. Mouth hanging open, drool wetting his lips, Jenks began to use the blood as paint.

He worked as if in a deep trance, slapping blood on the walls, dipping his hands in the pulp of Bradley's face, slapping more red on the walls. When there was enough paint on the walls he began to use his fingers to swirl the blood and smear it like some morbid styling of Van Gogh, only this wasn't a self-portrait—the face wasn't even recognizable, just a crimson smear.

Soon enough Jenks was finished. His hands hung at his sides, trembling.

A bubble gurgled from the blood puddle that was Bradley's face.

Jenks shuddered. He opened the door and left the park.

Ten minutes later the door opened again.

Dry leaves crunched beneath uncertain footsteps as Bradley stumbled out of the park. He held his ruined face up as if seeking guidance from the sun. One eye had been jellied into its fractured cavity and the other dangled over his cheek like a morbid Christmas tree ornament. With every step he became more certain of the direction in which he moved, as if some invisible beam guided him to his destiny.

No thoughts running through a mind punctured by splinters of skull, and yet Bradley's pace increased as his wet, sticky face was bathed in glorious sunlight. He moved forward, crossing streets by mere instinct, or perhaps fate, until he came upon a house he was only familiar with in passing. Everyone knew of Danny's house. It was the place where there seemed to be no rules, where Josh and his ilk could sit in the garage drinking beer and smoking weed, taunting their neighborhood peers with ugly slurs and mean-spirited jokes. As Bradley approached he couldn't smell the oily reek of the place that wafted from the garage like a warning, for his nose had become defunct. He couldn't smell the spilled beer and foul bong water, but deep within he knew he was at the right place.

Voices trickled into Bradley's blood-clogged ears, faint, worried voices:

"You gotta go to the hospital, man. Your hands are broken."

"I can't do that!"

"Can you move your fingers?"

"Fuck, it hurts!"

"Call 911, but don't do it here."

"Yeah, don't bring police here, man. Go home and get help."

"Fuck you!"

"Fuck me? Fuck you! What are you gonna do? You can't even move your damn fingers."

"What the fuck is that?"

115

The last comment was clearer, directed toward Bradley who stood in the driveway facing the open garage door where Josh, hands held out before him like damaged goods, stood arguing with his deadbeat friends. Bradley could feel their gaze upon him. His sense of hearing seemed amplified as he stood there with his head raised and cocked slightly. Sun glinted off the drying blood that filled the concave ruin where his nose and eyes had once been. His lower jaw was cocked at an odd angle, a few teeth jutting like random kernels on a gnawed cob of corn. The faceplate had been completely crushed in and pulped into a gooey mess caked over with a glossy patch of coagulated blood that oozed from rips and tears with fresh red drizzles.

Josh, eyes wide like he was tied up in a rattlesnake pit, said, "What the fuck?"

Danny cringed. "Jesus, dude! That's what you did to him? You're fucking crazy, man."

Josh stood just outside the garage door on the motor-oil-saturated driveway. His three friends, seated on an old grime-blackened and torn couch, scrambled to evacuate and avoid the grisly sight that was Bradley Jenkins. Danny, who had already been standing in his attempt to usher Josh away from his house and deal with his busted hands elsewhere, tripped over an extension cord and fell on his face, half in and half out of the garage. Before Joey and Mitch could make it out of the garage the large aluminum door came down like a guillotine, smashing Danny right on his back just above his tailbone. He screamed as his spine was fractured. His two friends inside the garage frantically tried to lift the door, but it was firmly clenched in place as if trying to sever Danny's torso. Danny just screamed and screamed, but was unable to move so much as a finger.

Witness to this horror, Josh made to flee, but tripped over his own feet. Instinctually he placed his hands out to catch his fall and, realizing his mistake, hit the ground hard. The pain from his smashed hands couldn't even be rivaled by the crack his nose made on the driveway as it broke and began gushing blood. He turned over onto his back and wept. Blood-spittle sprayed from his lips.

Bradley took several steps forward and hovered over his nemesis. Josh was *every* kid's nemesis. He was every bully personified. A terror of a human being with a future so bleak hope wasn't even a possibility.

Josh looked up at the thing towering over him. The thing he created. Blood ran down the sides of his face in red streams. Tears flooded his eyes like so many tears he had caused over the years, so much blood he'd drawn from easy targets and strong punches.

Bradley didn't even clench his fists. He reached up and palmed his own damaged face, grabbing the thick coagulation and pulling it away. Blood flowed freely in a sickening rush. Josh screamed as red rained over him. Bradley dropped to his knees. As Josh made a sloppy attempt at retreating from the hovering horror, Bradley grabbed the boy's arms and held him firm. Josh screamed as Bradley slowly dropped his bleeding face over Josh's. The bully screamed into the slick, wet void, drawing in Bradley's blood and choking. He squirmed and gurgled on the crimson flow, and then the squirming turned to violent trembling, and then Josh's body went still.

Bradley lifted his face from that of the boy who killed him and stood. Danny lay dead beneath the clenching maw of the aluminum garage door. A trickle of blood ran from his nose and mouth. Within the garage both Mitch and Joey yelled and pounded on the back of the aluminum door in metallic staccato. The sound of tools clinking together issued and the boys became silent. Clinking of shovels and the snip of hedge trimmers.

Muffled behind the door: "What the...?"

The tools clanked feverishly as the boys screamed, sounds of slashing and cutting and meat ripping and tearing, and then blood pooled from beneath the garage door, cascading around Danny's dead body.

Satisfied, Bradley turned and walked back to the park. No thoughts in his mind. Nothing to worry about. No bullies, no taunts and berating from his father. Nothing. Chirping birds drifted into his ears as dry leaves crunched under foot.

Bradley opened the door to the shunned restroom and entered his domain.

Diamond In The Rough
J. R. Park

I must have fallen asleep in front of the TV.

The fucker had ransacked my room before I'd woken up. Trashed the joint. Cheeky bastard even touched up his makeup before he left. God damn transvestite. Took the time to leave me a message. Thick, red lipstick words scrawled across the mirror:

Thank you Angel.
Take my advice.
Check out early.
Diamond x x

Angel's the name I use when I'm trying to impress, so I must have really liked this one.

My hangover turns last night into a soup of feelings and thought forms. Flashbacks hit me. His pretty smile and firm ass cut through the fog of regret, which rides through me like tidal surges, matching my nausea.

As I take in the carnage of the motel room a panic makes me clutch at my chest. My fingers dart around but are unable to feel my gold chain. My amulet.

Fuck.

The discovery of its theft drives me from my bed. The room spins at my sudden movement. I stumble into the bathroom and, leaning against the basin, scoop handfuls of water into my thirsty mouth.

I bundle my clothes into my rucksack in seconds, put my shoes on and stop to read his message one last time. I don't know what he knows, but his words read like a warning I'd be stupid to ignore.

I look past the words and see the dishevelled face of a man with a hangover. Last night's debauchery does not wear well on me. I should rest.

But as I check out and make my way across the car park, I see two cops heading to reception.

I don't have to be a genius to work out who they're after.

I keep changing: my hair, my beard, my clothes, my vehicle. But the chase never ends. It never will.

I place a pair of sunglasses on the bridge of my nose and kick start my bike.

America's a big place. Big enough for me to keep one step ahead.

But the lure of Mexico, the freedom on the other side of the border continues to call me.

I've been unconsciously heading further south since all this began. My travels resemble the whirring current of a draining bath. Perhaps my final destination has already been decided. Perhaps I had this all figured out from the start; destined to follow the inescapable pull of a new life in South America. Only I would be stupid enough to have a plan and not tell myself.

Maybe I'll should give in to the idea, ditch the bike, pick up a camper and a fake passport and look like a holiday maker.

The engine of the bike growls between my legs and I'm not ashamed at the arousal this induces.

Wherever I go, whatever I decide, first I've got to get that amulet back.

Reconnecting the dots of last night I begin retracing my steps, heading into each bar and hitting up the staff for information. I'm drawing a blank as I ask them about Diamond. Apparently six foot knockout transvestites are a dime a dozen in this neighbourhood. But they all suggest the same place, and although I've never heard of it, the mural of flames and she-devils outside the entrance of Big Reds does spark a glint of recognition.

Nightclubs always look a little out of sorts when viewed in the day time, but the location of Big Reds in the middle of an industrial trading estate make it look even weirder.

I bang on the door and a rat-faced man in a penguin suit answers. I ask if he knows Diamond.

The gentleman, whose name I later discover is Jack, is very amenable after a little persuasion.

With Jack left picking his teeth up off the sidewalk, I stroll into the dark hallway of Big Reds.

I was expecting the stillness of a deserted building, maybe the clink of glasses and the whirring of vacuum cleaners as the place was readied for another evening of hedonist revellers. So the blood curdling screams of anguish come as a surprise.

Following the sound but sticking close to the shadows I see a group of figures stood on the dancefloor surrounding a chair with a man wrapped in rope, screaming his head off. A bucket's been placed below him and as I make out rivulets of liquid pouring from the man's seat, I work out why. From the way my nose curls and my stomach contracts it's clear what the lumpy, viscous liquid is.

'You were right,' one of the encircling group turns to another, 'he did shit himself.'

My senses sharpen, adjusting to the darkness and filling in the gaps left by the blue and pink disco lights that swirl around the room to a soundless song.

The collar of the captured man's shirt begins to bulge as his screams turn to pathetic whispers. A dark shape emerges from underneath his shirt. Something stubby feeling the skin around his neck. The bulge grows bigger as the black blot crawls out from under his clothes. Eight legs of the biggest spider I have ever seen caress the warm, quivering flesh of his terrified cheek.

'Careful, Ruiz,' the largest of the men steps closer, kneeling so their eyes are level with his. 'The Goliath bird eating spider is the largest spider in the world. Those huge, four centimetre fangs can crush a mouse skull. Your skin ain't gonna be shit to it.'

The hulking arachnid slowly creeps up his cheek; its feet resting on his nose and forehead. Its front pedipalps explore his skin, caressing his eyebrows with a sinister curiosity. Even I feel an involuntary shiver as I watch this man live out his nightmare.

'When frightened she'll attack. She'll go for somewhere soft. Somewhere delicate. Somewhere where you're most vulnerable. Like your eyes.'

A low groan comes from the mouth of the man tied up.

'Steady now, Ruiz, you don't want to startle her.'

I watch them laugh as the large man stands up and pulls a blade from his suit jacket. Running the tip along the other man's thigh he maintains eye contact with his captive through the veil of hairy spider's legs, and calmly exerts pressure on the knife.

'Don't make a sound,' the big man grins with delight.

The blade cuts through the denim of Ruiz's jeans and his leg begins to quiver. Blood rises up through the slit and drips down his trousers, pouring in the bucket. It hits the shit at the bottom and sends a new plume of wretch-inducing stink through the club.

The big man's smile widens as he sinks the knife deeper. Ruiz is visibly shaking in his seat, struggling to remain mute.

'You don't want to spook the spider.' The fucker's enjoying this way too much.

Moving the blade towards his knee, I watch the big man ease the tip down behind the kneecap. The spider twitches, responding to the unsettling vibrations of the man desperately trying to suppress the pain.

'Oh, you're good, Ruiz.' The torturer is eerily calm, but I sense a growing impatience. The air thickens and goosebumps cover my body.

Lifting the knife, he pauses to smile then jabs again, this time twisting the blade. I hear the tip hit the bone. A howl of pain fills the nightclub. Digging at the back of the knee, the big man scrapes at the bone and levers the knee up; pulling it from his leg. Convulsing in agony, Ruiz is helpless as the spider raises its front legs then sinks its oversized fangs into the soft white of his right eye.

Ruiz's screams hit a new level of intensity as he shakes his head, but the harder he tries to throw the arachnid free the harder it grips; digging those teeth further and further into the oozing orb of his punctured eye.

'You fuck with us again, Ruiz,' the big man shouts, 'and next time it's your family, you understand?'

'John!' a voice calls behind me.

The big man turns.

'John! You got company.'

I recognise the wet speech of a man talking through his own blood. It's rat-faced Jack. He'd finished picking up his teeth and got his act together quicker than I thought.

Shit.

That spectacle of brutality had me entranced. Caught me napping like an idiot.

John sees me, as does his cronies. I step into the light. No point trying to hide now.

'I'm looking for Diamond,' I state, a toughness edged into my voice – to show a weakness to these cunts would be suicide.

'That so?' John tilts his head with genuine intrigue.

His cronies rush me. Brutes in business suits. I raise my fists ready for the fight. These fuckers aren't taking me down without a few bruises for themselves.

Swinging for the closest thug, I feel the satisfying crunch of his cheek bone beneath my knuckles. My senses sharpen as I smell his blood. I can practically taste it and my mouth fills with saliva. That's when I feel the sting of a pin-prick on my neck. I raise my hand to the pain but the damage is done. Whatever rat-faced Jack stuck me with works fast. My legs buckle beneath me and my rag doll body becomes a punch bag for the enraged thug I'd taken a swing at. His friends join in but my fading consciousness has already forgotten how to feel. Pain is nothing but a word.

The room darkens and the last thing I recall is the taste of blood in my mouth again. Only this time it's my own.

The ceiling and floor slowly separate; the joins dividing like melting caramel. Sounds bleed through from the soup of colours. The sounds become voices, distorted and indecipherable. Images emerge from the chaos and begin to settle. The sounds soon follow but for a while they mean nothing to me. I stare vacantly at the talking figures whilst I pull on the ropes around my wrists.

'….although he doesn't use his real name. Calls himself Angel.'

A smile threatens my blank expression as I clock the TV. He's gorgeous and I can't help but imagine sliding my hand up his short skirt and filling my mouth with his hard cock. It's then I realise the fantasy is based on more than my imagination. His name's Diamond and he's the transvestite I've been looking for.

'He's on the run,' Diamond explains to John as the big man studies my helpless form; tied to the chair in front of him. 'Came to America from England three years ago with his partner. There was a disturbance at their house. Neighbours called the police. Cops found his boyfriend chopped to pieces and launched a manhunt for Angel. Only the search threw up the discovery of more dead bodies. Trail went cold but they've been trying to track him ever since.'

'And how did you...?' The big man rubs his goatee with intrigue.

'The internet, honey; it's a wonderful thing. I met the gorgeous hunk last night. After a hard fuck he passed out. I was bored and couldn't sleep, so did a google search and found all manner of shit about him. I figured I'd let the cops chase him out of town. Gave them a tip off and him a head start. It was only fair.'

'Really? You call that piece of trash gorgeous?'

'He's a rugged. A bit of rough. Like Hugh Jackman or someone.'

'Diamond...' I slur my speech.

'Oh hush, darling, the drugs haven't worn off yet.' He smiles at me.

My eyes scan the room. The three thugs are nursing wounds, mementoes of my fists, and staring at me with smouldering grudges. Rat-faced Jack stands to one side, curious to watch my fate but clearly not keen to participate unless he absolutely has to.

'Hello, Angel,' the big man steps forward. 'My name's John, Carlito John. I don't take too kindly to you coming in here. My associates let me use this place out of hours, for no charge and in good faith. I can't leave this place in a mess, so need to tidy up after myself. You understand? My colleagues here are especially pissed about our encounter after your little commotion. It's one thing to upset me, but it's another to upset them. So that's two mistakes you've made today, already. You listen to me, answer my questions and that'll keep you from making a third. Got it?'

The smell of his breath as he leans closer tightens my stomach. I can make out the odour of his breakfast, the mint he sucked on an hour ago, and the adrenalin that currently courses through his bloodstream.

My senses are sharpening.

Becoming unnaturally heightened.

Shit.

'What are you doing here? And what do you want with Diamond?' Carlito John asks, his voice threatening in its serenity.

'My necklace. My amulet.' My voice finds its strength. I almost dare a smile. 'I need my amulet.'

'This thing?' Diamond pulls the charm from his handbag. 'Beautiful, isn't it?'

He admires the Native American patterns that interweave an iridescent stone, then shows it to Carlito John.

'What a piece of garbage,' the big man scoffs. 'You interrupt me and cause a commotion for this cheap crap?'

'It's not crap,' I explain. 'I need it.'

A jab to my face stops my words. I spit blood from my mouth as I watch Carlito John smile at his handiwork.

'It's an amulet. A charm from a shaman.'

Another fist silences me again. This one splitting my cheek.

I pause for a moment to gather my senses.

'Please, you don't understand, I need it before-' Carlito John punches me a third time, this time I hear my nose crack.

The pain stokes a growing rage and I feel my muscles strain against the rope around me.

'I'm tired of this whiny piece of shit. He's a loser. A fucking nobody. Boys, have your revenge. Do your worst.'

Carlito John steps backwards, indicating it's play time for his apes.

They don't need a second invitation. Even rat-faced Jack takes the cue and launches at me with fists and boots.

'Diamond,' I try to call amidst the barrage but the wind is knocked from my lungs and my face is full of knuckles.

The chair rocks underneath me. I feel my shirt rip from my back and realise it must be nightfall. I've run out of time.

My chest expands and my toes push against my shoes. As my fingers crack and extend, the nails thickening to claw-like points, my binds thread and snap against the strain of my increasing bulk. The chair cracks and splinters under my growing mass and my attackers yield, mesmerised by the supernatural sight of my changing form.

I stand above them, pushing seven foot and still growing. White fur coats my body. My eyes change to a piercing yellow. I go to shout, to tell them to run, but my voice has already reduced to the roar of an animal.

I wonder what they must be thinking. They didn't give me a chance to explain about the car accident. The grieving mother. Her revenge with an arcane curse.

My face swells and twists into a protruding snout, forcing my jaw wider as my teeth grow into elongated points.

The thugs step back in shock as I tower over them. Rat-faced Jack turns to run but I pounce on him, sinking my claws into his back as I knock him to the floor. The poor bastard is still screaming as I grip his spine and pull it from his torso. Stamping on his head, I watch his skull crack and his brains ooze out over my feet.

By the time I turn around the thugs are running towards me. One pulls out a gun but I swipe a claw and he's left with bloody stump that's geysering out grue. A second slash, this time across his stomach, sends his intestines slopping to the floor like a split bag of sausages.

Another comes at me but I open his windpipe with ease. Enjoying the shower of warm blood his body soaks me in, I grasp his head and place it in my mouth, allowing my teeth to slowly sink into his face. I hear the wet gargles of his protest and savour the sound for a few seconds before silencing him with the satisfying crunch of his splintering skull.

The last thug picks up a table and hurls it at my direction, but I bat it away with ease. He turns blindly and runs into a large, glass tank. He falls and the tank lands on him, smashing across his back and shattering; slicing his skin to ribbons. The bird-eating spider, now released from its capture, crawls over the prone man. He cowers on the floor as the arachnid creeps across his chest, and I begin to enjoy the sweet scent of his terror.

'You a Wendigo?' he burbles through his tears.

I'm impressed with his knowledge of monsters, but it doesn't save him from my bloodlust.

A scream rings out as I chew on his freshly severed arm. I turn to watch Carlito John throw Diamond to the floor and run out, locking the exit behind him.

The door is nothing but firewood to me. I could easily smash through it and chase him to his death, but my instincts aren't shaped by revenge, they are moulded by an insatiable hunger. A hunger that can only be quelled by human flesh.

Crouching on all fours, I gallop across the nightclub and pounce at Diamond. He falls to the floor and I stand over him. Blood pours from the severed arm still in my mouth, splattering my next victim.

Diamond scrabbles around in the growing pool of gore that drenches him. His fingers find his handbag.

'Here, you want it so bad!' he screams and throws something at me.

As the amulet strikes my chest I already begin to feel its neutralising power. I instinctively grab it, clutching the charm as I fight the creature within.

Spitting out the severed arm, I can feel my strength weaken; my body shrinks, and my thoughts regain some form of clarity. I crawl to a corner of the club and curl up, allowing the ancient artefact to suppress the arcane curse of the bestial Wendigo.

For a few moments there is nothing but silence. My eyes are closed, although I can feel the room spinning and my nausea returns. As my senses ebb towards a manageable equilibrium the quiet is broken by the sound of high heels.

'What the fuck?' Diamond approaches me, wiping blood from his eyes.

I turn to face him and watch the gore drip from his skirt.

'You okay now?' he asks.

'As long as I have the amulet,' I reply.

'Fucking creeps. They deserve what they got. Let's get out of here,' he says, taking my arm and helping me to my feet. 'We'll use the fire escape. Head back to mine. Take a shower.'

The thought of his naked body, wet and soapy and pressed against me forces a stir in the ragged remains of my pants.

I'm hard the whole ride back to his apartment and we're fucking the moment the taps turn on.

For a moment I think about Carlito John and wonder if I should hunt him down or leave him alone. I'd soon disappear, and he wouldn't waste his time looking for me. Would he? Aside from him, this beautiful transvestite is the only witness connecting me to the massacre in Big Reds. As Diamond's huge dick fills my ass I consider letting him live. Then I think better of it.

Virtue of Stagnant Waters
Monica J. O'Rourke

Tommy Kirten had been dead, by lethal injection, for more than five years. At first he'd left a wake of survivors but later destroyed all traces of evidence—except for the journals that ultimately resulted in his undoing.

Nicole Beauchamp had closely followed media reports, along with most of the world, scrolling through Facebook and Reddit feeds and various news sites to glean what bits of information anyone was willing to share. As a reporter, she knew what to look for and what to ignore, sifting through fact and innuendo, trying to patchwork some semblance of an article. Nicole knew she had to one day tell the story.

She couldn't tell *her* story—not yet; her wounds were just too deep.

But she could learn so much from them.

"I'm writing an article," she told them when she introduced herself by phone and tried to arrange the interviews. By the time she finished blurting "Tommy"— three of the eight survivors screamed or cursed before terminating the call.

But Victim #1 (though technically she was the fourth woman to accept the invitation), Lisa, agreed to meet. When Nicole used the words "victim," "survivor," or "*closure*," it was usually a done deal.

They met in a coffee shop that was way too loud for the small number of customers inside.

Lisa wore baggy sweats and a baggy sweater, seeming to hide a latitude of sins that likely existed only in her mind. Nicole noted the pulled-back hair, the makeup-less face, the slumped-shoulder demeanor.

"How long has it been?" Nicole asked, the rest of the question unasked but understood.

"Nine years," Lisa whispered, clearing her throat. "Nine years, three months, fourteen days…"

Nicole nodded, sipped her coffee. "Okay if I record this?"

Lisa nodded.

Nicole pressed record on the microcassette recorder. She crossed her ankle over her knee and scratched her foot. "Tell me what happened. Go straight through it; I'll save any questions for the end."

"Fine." Lisa looked around, seeming reluctant to start. She sighed gently, as if changing her mind midstream, and glanced at the floor.

The wait was an eternity for Nicole, who resisted the urge to glance at the time on her phone. If she had positioned this interview better, Nicole would be facing the clock hanging on the wall behind her.

Lisa sipped coffee from a cup that was held by trembling fingers. As she exhaled, her head dropped a few inches, as if she was about to take a nap. "I didn't notice him at first. He pulled up next to me in his car. Reports about him being a killer hadn't made the news yet. I had no reason…"—her breath hitched—"to suspect anything. No reason to worry. He had such a nice smile. He was this fatherly looking guy. Brown hair. Small glasses. He was so young and looked so innocent. His car was so clean inside and out. He just seemed so…normal."

Nicole nodded, eyes riveted on her subject. "Go on," she whispered.

"'Where are you headed?' he asked me. I still didn't suspect anything. People were always offering rides in that neighborhood."

"Where were you coming from?"

"Grocery shopping. I was heading home. It wasn't that far, and my car was in the shop. He said, 'I live close, on Maple,' and offered me a ride.

"He came at me from behind." Her hands, wrapped around the paper cup, trembled. "I was already in his car. He…"

A few moments passed. Nicole wasn't sure what to do. "Are you okay?"

She whispered, "Some minutes are better than others."

Nicole was surprised by this. It had been more than nine years since she'd escaped, after all, and Kirten was dead. She wondered how much longer Lisa's recovery would take. After all, she'd survived. She was better off than quite a few other victims.

After a long, awkward pause, Nicole asked, "Do you need to stop now?"

Lisa mentally consulted with her cup of coffee. "No."

Nicole reached across the table and gently patted her hand. "You're very brave."

Lisa lifted her eyes, clearly recognizing Nicole's patronizing tone. "Why are you writing this article anyway? You don't seem terribly sympathetic, if I'm being honest here."

Nicole jerked her hand back and stared at the wretchedly boring seascape on the wall. "I'm sorry," she muttered. "I'm doing this…I need closure."

She took a long, slow sip from her cup and continued. "You see...my child didn't survive. I was hoping...was, well, by speaking to some of the survivors...maybe I would learn, you know, what happened there. To, to, you know, understand what you went through..." She dropped her head and stared at scratches in the tabletop.

"I'm so sorry," Lisa said, inhaling deeply. "Oh my God. Oh my God."

"It's okay," Nicole whispered. "We're in this together."

After a slight pause: "He grabbed me from behind," Lisa said, much stronger now, as if determined to share this story.

Screaming seemed to make it worse. Seemed to excite him more.

"Please!" she begged, her voice hoarse. "*Please don't!*"

"Don't what?" he asked, leaning in to her prone body lying on the metal table, his hot breath on her cheek, neck, breast... "Don't what?" he asked again, his fingers inside her cunt, her ass, working both holes, flexing, making fists, jamming deep inside her.

"You see," he said breathily, pulling out his hands and wiping blood and shit on the towel draped over his shoulder, "there's nothing better than the *feel* of a woman...to be inside her, to touch her and dig in deep. You know what I mean?"

She shook her head and moaned. "Please stop! Please..." she whimpered.

He tore off a piece of duct tape and slapped it over her mouth. "I'll miss the screams, but I can live without the begging."

She threw her head back and forth, screaming into the gag, unspoken pleas tearing from her throat.

He lifted Lisa's chained hands above her head and fastened the chain to the meat hook from the ceiling, pulling her up and off the table. Her naked body stood before him, and she tried to twist away, but he separated her feet and chained her ankles to the floor.

"Stop twisting."

But she wouldn't. When she forced herself to stop, her body took over and still tried to pull away from him, even though she knew the attempts were useless. She couldn't stop.

"Stop twisting," he repeated, this time more quietly.

She stopped, but as soon as he moved, so did she.

He wheeled in a table covered with an assortment of nightmarish gadgets: knives, scissors, scalpels, nipple clamps, battery cables, pliers, whips...other things she never knew existed. Things that made her scream and twist again, things that made her suddenly pray for death.

"I'm not *fucking* with you," he growled in her ear. He picked up a device that looked like a pizza cutter but with jagged, serrated edges. He ran it lightly across his palm, seemed to caress the tool, but then placed it back on the table. Instead, he picked up a battery jumper cable and clamped it on her nipple. This nipple clamp wasn't meant for sex play but for attaching to a car's battery. The tight cable bit fiercely into her flesh, severing the nipple halfway from her body. She screeched into her gag, throwing back her head, hysterical sobs shaking her, sweat pouring off her body.

He left it all dangling there, one bloody squirting pulpy mess, her shrieking so horrendously into the duct tape that she came close to popping a blood vessel in her eye.

He finally removed the clamp, her damaged nipple swinging on a grisly string of shriveled flesh. He slapped another piece of duct tape across the mangled mess.

The pain dulled to a throbbing, raw ache.

"Next time I tell you to do something, you'd better fucking do it."

She nodded. And nodded. Her body trembled, but it was nothing she could control. It was like a light electrical pulse throughout her body.

He approached her from behind and wrapped his hands around her waist, both palms pressing into her stomach. "Lean forward," he said, and she tried, but her movements were limited. He didn't seem to care. Seconds later his fingers were again inside her ass, and she smelled the tang of her blood more strongly now, more than just from the damaged nipple...he seemed to be using it to lube her ass.

Seconds later his fingers were out and his cock was in, his balls slapping against her. He pushed hard against her back, trying to force her to bend even further, his dick painfully slamming against the inside of her asshole, trying to force its way into her colon. His pulsing intensified, pounding harder and harder and she screamed into the duct tape gag, the pain ripping through her body until she thought she would puke inside her gag and drown on her own vomit.

He slowed finally, and she felt a quick sense of relief until the pounding started again, harder than ever, until she practically tried to climb her own arm to get away.

With one final, violent shudder he ejaculated inside her, his cock shaking as if filled with electricity, and, finally spent, he withdrew his dick.

She tried to drop to her knees, but the chains kept her suspended far enough from the floor. She dangled from her wrists, her body exhausted and in agony.

He approached her and lifted her chin with one hand. "I want to remove your gag. Can I trust you?"

She barely nodded, too exhausted to move any more than that.

"If you beg me for anything again, I'll cut off your other nipple and feed it to you."

Again she nodded. She knew he meant it.

He lay her on the table and attached her chains to the sides.

"Sweet dreams," he said, turning off the lights.

The room was windowless, and other than a barely discernable sliver of light under the door, it was utter blackness.

Every nerve ending came alive, a level of intensity she wasn't expecting. Her damaged nipple screamed out in pain. She heard her own breathing, jagged and rough, slipping from her nostrils but also rattling thickly in her lungs. Sleep was almost impossible, but eventually a fever-sleep overtook her, forced her to close her eyes,

and despite the pain and thirst and fear, she slipped into a level of unawareness, if only for a brief period.

She woke to ice water being dumped on her head. Her horrible thirst was barely quenched. She turned her head, coughing and retching, water dripping from her nose and mouth, fighting desperately to catch her breath and clear her lungs.

He unchained her feet and quickly moved between her legs. She resisted, pulling her knees together. A second later she realized what she had done and quit fighting him, but judging the furious and surprised look on his face, it was probably too late.

He spit into his hand and massaged the phlegm into her pussy. He spat again and lubed his cock. He crawled up the stainless steel table and shoved his cock inside her, pumping madly, his head slightly thrown back. She could see the madness on his face, the pure hatred as his features reddened from his cheeks to his forehead to the tips of his ears.

The rapes went on for several days before he inexplicably unchained her and dumped her in the middle of the woods.

"I was one of his first," Lisa said into the edge of her empty cup. "The police think he escalated after that."

Nicole nodded. *He sure did,* she thought.

"He let me go," she whispered, "but he killed so many others." Now the tears dripped down her cheeks, the weight of her story crashing down on her.

"And you don't know why he let you go."

136

"No…he let me go…and there were at least three others." Her voice was quiet, her face downturned, like a petulant child being punished. Like a stroke victim no longer in control of her features. "H-he…" Her words were becoming gibberish.

Nicole knew the interview was over. "Survivor guilt," she said quietly, and Lisa shrugged, neither agreeing nor disagreeing.

Nicole glanced down at her notes and suddenly became excited at the material she had captured.

Nicole met with three other victims. It was hard to imagine anyone had suffered worse than Lisa. But she had taken careful notes. Such detailed notes. As soon as she expressed sympathy toward them, Nicole discovered, the more they opened up. Amazing.

One more series of questions for Lisa, the last survivor.

"The thing with the boats?" Nicole asked.

"What boats?"

"You don't know about his experiments? Did Tommy ever mention boats to you?"

"What are you talking about?" She sounded like she was getting annoyed with Nicole's questions.

She realized Lisa couldn't have known. Nicole had acquired things the police didn't know existed. Some of Tommy's journals were never made public. Had never been found by anyone—until Nicole got her hands on them. And he'd kept meticulous records.

His journals were so revealing, had told the police and investigators so much—the details of each assault, his vivid descriptions of the joy his suffering victims had given him. Their admission as evidence at the trial (over his defense attorney's strong objections) had resulted in his ultimate demise.

If only they had known about *this* journal. It revealed so much more; his thoughts, motivations, instructions, laid out in diary form. They outlined the details of his psychological journey toward pure sadism as he pursued a fulfillment based on pure, raw suffering. Never intended the world to see. Never wanted anyone at all to see.

So many lives wasted, destroyed. So many victims. So little empathy.

It was easiest to hold them here, a place the police still had not discovered. A place, strangely enough, of serenity and beauty, where the enraged cries of the loons and winsome, yearning wolf howls mixed so smoothly with the plaintive cries of his girls.

He'd already had his fun at the main house, and he realized just how much he enjoyed what he was doing. But it had gotten dangerous there—too many had escaped or been released—so he moved to the cabin in the woods. His fatal mistake had been to return to the place in the city where the cops had been waiting.

But for now...this place...so magical. Almost invisible, he believed.

The stagnant little pond behind the cabin was an especially nice touch. Perhaps a ten-minute canoe glide around the circumference, Tommy spent many afternoons observing his experiment, undisturbed by the outside world, cries and screams of agonies going unheard across the vast wilderness. A random hiker would be unable to pinpoint the exact location of the screams...

He started with one. He wasn't sure how many he could maintain and wanted to begin.

He began several weeks ago by creating his boats, which was simply piling one carved-out canoe on top of the other. It resembled a giant oval walnut when both halves were joined. His makeshift watercraft was indeed seaworthy and waterproof, he discovered after testing.

Then he quickly found his girl.

Several miles away, he caught the hiker peeing in the woods. She was easy to overtake, squatting in the bushes with her pants around her ankles. She squeaked when he grabbed her from behind, covering her face with the chloroformed rag. Not that knocking her out was actually necessary—no witnesses—but he really didn't relish the idea of an annoying kicking and screaming girl to have to deal with.

He set her up in the basement, tied to the table, but he kept her comfortable, feeding her a delicious concoction of milk and honey. She refused to eat, of course, so he force-fed her.

The room was dimly lit in an attempt to keep her calm, but nothing seemed to work. Not that it mattered. Very little upset him.

"It's good," he said in a singsong way, as if feeding a toddler. "Here—yum."

She sobbed and coughed and cried in a hiccupping way, "Pl-e-he-he-hease! Let me go! I won't tell!"

He was taken aback. Tell who? They were in the middle of nowhere! He laughed at her. "Open your mouth."

"Pl-e-he-*hease!*"

He shoved the spoon into her mouth and she coughed, milk and honey spraying across the room, his shirt. Still didn't annoy him. There was plenty of time.

Within three days she had barely consumed enough milk and honey to make him happy. Enough dicking around with this one.

He slammed the door and locked it, putting the key in his pocket, and turned up the lights so he could see what he was doing.

The girl was sitting on the far corner of the bed, her knees pulled up to her chest.

"Come here," he demanded. When she didn't move, he unbuckled his belt. "I only ask once. After that, you'll be sorry you ignored me."

Perhaps she was testing him, but he repeated his command—and a repeat was a rare, rare occurrence—and when she didn't budge, he pulled his belt through the loops, folding it in his hands.

He raised it high above his head and slapped her hard across the legs. She screamed and tried to crawl closer to the wall. He grabbed her ankle and yanked, dragging her across the mattress. Flipping her on her stomach, he pinned her down, holding her across her back with a meaty forearm, and slapped the shit out of her with the belt.

She sobbed and wailed and tried desperately to pull away, screaming for mercy.

He finally stopped, keeping her pinned down, and said breathily, "You have no place to go. There's no escape. If you continue to disobey me, I will beat you bloody until you obey. Do you understand?" he roared.

"Yes!" she shrieked.

After that, things went much more smoothly.

He stripped her naked and left her sitting quietly on the bed. Several times a day he fed her bowls of milk and honey. She sobbed through most of it, but anytime she complained he threatened to beat or rape her. He never did rape this one ... he wanted her for other purposes.

On her fifth day of captivity he laid her out on the bed and bound her hands and feet. She cried throughout the entire thing, but he never hurt her.

He applied honey all over her body, generously smearing great amounts on her eyes, nose, mouth, pussy, and ass. She resisted, but only until he cleared his throat, and she knew enough to stop fighting him.

He carried her outside and brought her to the back of the house, laying her on the grass beside the pond.

Glistening and dripping with honey, the girl squirmed against her bindings, trying to move onto her side, possibly hoping to get to her elbows and knees and perhaps attempt an escape. But Tommy knew how weak she was, and even if she managed to stand, she wasn't going anywhere.

The hollowed-out boats lay at the side of the pond. He flipped the top half, revealing two boats. Inside one he had placed a pillow—for leverage, not comfort—and returned to his girl, his science experiment.

Now she started kicking and screaming, perhaps believing he was going to drown her. He placed his large hand over her face and shushed her, blocking her air passages. She instantly stopped fighting.

"I'm not going to kill you," he said gently. "I promise."

He laid her inside the boat and untied her feet, pulling her legs apart, placing each ankle in a hole on opposite sides, tying the feet to bolts in the sides. He did the same with her arms, pulling them out straight to the sides until she looked crucified. He positioned her head carefully on the pillow.

He pulled the second boat on top of her, securing the two halves, only her head, hands, and feet exposed.

He pushed the boat away from shore but anchored it, allowing it to travel only a few feet away.

Then he waited.

It happened quicker than he had expected. Within hours the girl started screaming ... simple cries of discomfort at first, quickly growing into squeals of pain and then pure anguish. He sat at the edge of the pond and watched various species of insect take turns sampling her exposed, honey-smeared flesh. She was attacked at different times by water striders, mayflies, dragonflies, damselflies, mosquitoes, horseflies, giant waterbugs, maggot flies, hornets, wasps, and bees, biting, stinging, burrowing into flesh, consuming the vast amounts of explosive diarrhea her milk and honey diet had produced. The stench of her feces overpowered all smells around the pond.

Soon the pond was alive with the constant humming, buzzing drone of hundreds of insects consuming their victim, working their way under her skin, into hollowed cavities created by other insects. The girl's screams had subsided to a constant low moan, as if a record stuck on repeat, the only sound coming from her besides the creatures feeding on flesh and honey. Her face was no longer visible beneath a layer of flies, their maggot offspring creating a squirming layer on her skin. Tommy was sure she no longer had the strength to lift her head to shoo the flies away.

He had stopped feeding her. After five days of watching her slowly being eaten alive, and keeping her alive by force-feeding her more honey and some water, he decided to let her die.

There were always others he could try this on.

The next morning he went to check on her. The exposed body parts were unrecognizable, looking instead like solid insects. He couldn't tell if she was still alive. He couldn't even tell if she was still in the boat. If he'd bothered learning her name, he might have called out to her now.

Using the rope attached to the anchor, he pulled the boat ashore, the droning of the bugs growing louder and louder, the stench of shit and rotting flesh making his eyes water.

He gingerly unlatched the two boat halves. It took several attempts to flip the top over; they were practically glued together with honey and what he could only imagine were bodily fluids and excrement from God knew what.

He staggered away from the boat for a moment, his hand covering his mouth in shock. This was unlike anything he could have imagined. His bowels stirred in excitement, and he hunkered down a few feet away to watch the activity. After so much research, it was fascinating to see this process in action.

Her body was virtually alive with swarming insects; not one inch of her was untouched. She was bloated with gases and had become quite attractive to a variety of insects. Young maggots, moving en masse to preserve heat, traveled throughout her body, secreting digestive enzymes and tearing tissues with their mouth hooks.

Rats had burrowed their way in through the shallow end of the boat and had scattered only when he separated the boats. But some had also tunneled their way inside her body and frantically searched for ways to escape. One clawed and chewed its way through her groin, finally appearing in a fresh hole in her twat, looking like the world's hairiest and most disgusting newborn. It lifted its small head and blinked its beady eyes as if discovering its life for the first time before disappearing beneath the woman's corpse.

Tommy laughed. The websites never mentioned vermin, only bugs. Fascinating.

He was a few feet away but smelled the body clearly, a distinct chemical cocktail formed by hundreds of volatile organic compounds. He could detect the smell of fruit—apples, cherries, even raspberries—but the most powerful underlying smell for him was a sweet, delicious aroma of honey. He glanced at the mounds of diarrhea in various stages of decomposition and dryness and rushed back into the house. A few minutes later he returned carrying a barbecue spatula with an extended handle and a large plastic mixing bowl. Carefully reaching into the feces, avoiding the swarms of insects, he scooped up as much as he could and deposited it into the bowl, repeating a few times until it contained a decent amount. He wasn't sure yet what he was going to do with the diarrhea, but he expected it to taste amazing. Sweet, tangy …

After pushing the bowl aside, far from the boat, he resumed studying her. It was tempting to wash away the bugs with a hose to see what her remains looked like, but he didn't want to disturb their amazing ecosystem. For now, anyway.

The rate of decay had increased even in the short amount of time he'd begun watching, and more and more types of insects seemed to arrive: blowflies, flesh flies, beetles, which seemed to be attacking the maggots more than the corpse. The maggots were everywhere, consuming her surface, but he could also seem them under her skin.

Her flesh had turned gangrenous in parts, the skin mottled gray and green, small parts blackening.

He wondered at what point she had begun to rot away while still alive, spending her final hours or days in horrifying agony.

That was unclear. Next time he would pay much closer attention to the process in the boats.

Nicole unlocked the front door. She was convinced no one knew about this location, not even the police. It had never been in Tommy's name—he was too clever for that.

She'd managed to keep their relationship separate. No one had ever questioned her. She wasn't kidding when she'd told Lisa, "My child didn't survive."

Only Lisa never suspected Tommy was Nicole's child.

Nicole entered the house with her bags of supplies. She'd been shopping … and her list had been thorough. She wondered if she'd have the strength to build additional boats, but she could work with one victim at a time.

If only Tommy had left greater details about how the diarrhea had tasted. But she'd have to figure that out for herself.

Nicole went down to the basement where Lisa was chained up and gagged. It was time to resume her son's experiments.

Contributors

Glenn Rolfe is an author from the haunted woods of New England. He has studied Creative Writing at Southern New Hampshire University, and continues his education in the world of horror by devouring the novels of Stephen King, Ronald Malfi, Jack Ketchum, and many others. He and his wife, Meghan, have three children, Ruby, Ramona, and Axl. He is grateful to be loved despite his weirdness. He is a Splatterpunk Award nominee and the author of BECOMING, BLOOD AND RAIN, THE HAUNTED HALLS, CHASING GHOSTS, ABRAM'S BRIDGE, THINGS WE FEAR, and the collections, A BOX FULL OF MONSTERS, OUT OF RANGE, SLUSH and LAND OF BONES. Check out his latest novel, THE WINDOW.

Ryan Harding is the author of GENITAL GRINDER and co-author of REINCARNAGE with Jason Taverner, both from *Deadite Press*, co-author of the Splatterpunk Award-winning HEADER 3 with Edward Lee and 1000 SEVERED DICKS with Matt Shaw. GENITAL

GRINDER was published in Poland by *Dom Horroru* as BLASFEMIA. He contributed to the multi-author collaborations SIXTY-FIVE STIRRUP IRON ROAD and THE DEVIL'S GUESTS. His stories have also appeared in the anthologies *Year's Best Hardcore Horror Volume 3, Masters of Horror, DOA 3, Into Painfreak, In Laymon's Terms*, and *Excitable Boys;* the chapbooks *Partners in Chyme* (with Edward Lee), *A Darker Dawning* and *A Darker Dawning 2: Reign in Black*; and the magazines *Splatterpunk* and *The Magazine of Bizarro Fiction*. Upcoming projects include a novel with Bryan Smith and the sequel to REINCARNAGE with Jason Taverner.

Lydian Faust is a writer of horror and dark fiction. She is also a painter who likes to lay it on thick. Ms. Faust lives in one of the murder capitals of the United States of America. Her hobbies include nachos and alien conspiracy theories.

Ryan C. Thomas is an award-winning journalist and editor living in San Diego, California. He is the author of 13 novels (including the cult classic, THE SUMMER I DIED), numerous novellas and short stories, and can often be found in the bars around Southern California playing rockabilly guitar. When he is not writing or rocking out, he is at home with his wife, son, daughter, two dogs and cat watching really bad B-movies.

Michelle Garza and Melissa Lason are better known as the Sisters of Slaughter for their work in the horror genre. They have been published by *Thunderstorm books, Sinister Grin Press* and *Bloodshot Books*. Their debut novel, MAYAN BLUE, was nominated for a Bram Stoker Award. Their most recent work is SILVERWOOD: THE DOOR with Brian Keene, Richard Chizmar, Stephen Kozeniewski and Tony Valenzuela which launched in October 2018 through *Serialbox*.

Chad Lutzke lives in Michigan with his wife and children. For over two decades, he has been a contributor to several different outlets in the independent music and film scene, offering articles, reviews, and artwork. He has written for *Famous Monsters of Filmland, Rue Morgue, Cemetery Dance*, and *Scream* magazine. He's had a few dozen stories published, and some of his books include: OF FOSTER HOMES & FLIES, WALLFLOWER, STIRRING THE SHEETS, SKULLFACE BOY, and OUT BEHIND THE BARN co-written with John Boden. Lutzke's work has been praised by authors Jack Ketchum, Stephen Graham Jones, James Newman, and his own mother.

Saul Bailey lives in North Devon, where suicide is too scary, and alcoholism too expensive, leaving writing as the only way to keep the monsters from the door.

Nathan Robinson lives in Scunthorpe, England. He's contributed to over twenty different anthologies so far, with lots more on the horizon. His crime thriller TOP OF THE HEAP was adapted in a podcast by *Pseudopod* to rave reviews. STARERS, released by *Severed Press* in 2012 gained much praise, with fans hungry for a sequel. His novella KETCHUP ON EVERYTHING was released in 2014 to rave reviews, as was his short story collection DEVIL LET ME GO. His novella, MIDWAY was released by *Severed Press* in 2015, followed by CALDERA in 2016. CHUM is his fifth story published by *Splatterpunk Zine*.

Alessandro Manzetti is a Bram Stoker Award–winning author and editor of horror fiction and dark poetry whose work has been published extensively in Italian, including novels, short and long fiction, poetry, essays, and collections. English publications include his novel NARAKA – THE ULTIMATE HUMAN BREEDING, the collections THE GARDEN OF DELIGHT, THE MASSACRE OF THE MERMAIDS, THE MONSTER, THE BAD AND THE UGLY (with Paolo Di Orazio) and the poetry collections NO MERCY, EDEN UNDER-GROUND, WAR (with Marge Simon), SACRIFICIAL NIGHTS (with Bruce Boston), and VENUS INTER-VENTION (with Corrine De Winter). His stories and poems have appeared in Italian, American, and UK magazines and anthologies. He won the Bram Stoker Award in 2016 and was five times a nominee. He was also nominated for the Splatterpunk Award 2018 and other awards. He edited the anthologies *The Beauty of Death Vol. 1*, *The Beauty of Death Vol. 2 – Death by Water* (with Jodi Renee Lester) and *Monsters of Any Kind* (with Daniele Bonfanti). He is the CEO & Founder of *Independent Legions Press*, and an active member of the Horror Writers Association. He lives in Trieste, Italy.

Robert Essig is the author of several novels including DEATH OBSESSED, IN BLACK and PEOPLE OF THE ETHEREAL REALM. He has published several novellas, nearly 100 short stories and edited two small press anthologies. Robert lives with his family in Southern California.

JR Park is a writer of horror fiction, and was described by DLS Reviews as "A much needed shot in the arm for gritty pulp horror". Using pulp-horror as his base palate, he likes to experiment with structure and narrative to produce something different. His extreme horror novella UPON WAKING saw him try to redress the gender balance in the slasher genre, and saw *Scream* magazine saying "his mind must be the darkest place in the universe". Other books include THE EXCHANGE (Alice In Wonderland meets Reservoir Dogs meets H.P. Lovecraft), MAD DOG (a werewolf in a prison break), PUNCH (a love letter to the slasher golden age) and TERROR BYTE (Guy N Smith meets Philip K Dick). He worked with Matt Shaw to produce POSTAL, a blood-drenched commentary on society, was Assistant Director on the horror film *Monster* & co-runs the *Sinister Horror Company*.

Monica J. O'Rourke has published more than one hundred short stories in magazines and anthologies, such as *CLICKERS FOREVER: A TRIBUTE TO J. F. GONZALEZ, Postscripts, Nasty Piece of Work, Fangoria,* and *The Mammoth Book of the Kama Sutra.* She is the author of POISONING EROS, written with Wrath James White, SUFFER THE FLESH, WHAT HAPPENS IN THE DARKNESS, and the collection IN THE END, ONLY DARKNESS. Her books and stories have been published in Germany, Greece, Poland, and Russia. She is a freelance editor and book coach.

32851415R00094

Printed in Poland
by Amazon Fulfillment
Poland Sp. z o.o., Wrocław